PURGATORY

KEN BRUEN

ISIS
LARGE PRINT
Oxford

Copyright © Ken Bruen, 2013

First published in Great Britain 2013
by
Transworld Ireland
a Division of Transworld Publishers

Published in Large Print 2014 by ISIS Publishing Ltd.,
7 Centremead, Osney Mead, Oxford OX2 0ES
by arrangement with
Transworld Ireland
an Imprint of The Random House Group Ltd.

The moral right of the author has been asserted

CIP data is available for this title from the British Library

ISBN 978–0–7531–9294–8 (hb)
ISBN 978–0–7531–9295–5 (pb)

Printed and bound in Great Britain by
T. J. International Ltd., Padstow, Cornwall

For Michael and Ollie Crowe, Derek Hynes

Prologue

The skateboarders had that peculiar blend of Irish self-consciousness, dumb persistence. The uniquely good weather in early January had led to a makeshift ramp that was ambitiously steep and high. The Council would have removed it but had its hands full with the Occupiers, who had a large tent perched to the left side of Eyre Square.

The skateboarders kept the locals from lynching the Council over

water,

refuse,

home,

and just about all damn other charges.

Three Guards were deemed sufficient to watch the growing crowd for what was rumoured to be a spectacular attempt.

A double flip, *mid-air* from Joseph, a sixteen-year-old whizz flyer from Tuam. He was small, undistinguished, with the revamped grunge look that owed more to the new poverty than to fashion. Quiet seeped from him as he took his run at the ramp. A slight *aah* from the crowd as he accelerated faster than they'd expected,

3

then he was airborne high above the ramp, left the board, was mid-turn when the single shot rang out.

He seemed to hang for a moment, the top right side of his brain scattering in a slow mist, then a loud scream from the crowd as his body hurled to the concrete.

Two people were hurt in the panic.

A skater had the presence of mind to steal the almost-famous board.

Part 1

The Men

1

"Your crazy daughter is on our shortlist."
"There's nothing wrong with her."
"She talks to people who aren't there."
"No she doesn't, she only listens."

Carol O'Connell, author of *The Chalk Girl*

My life seemed to have reached a time of calm. New home, new habits (ish), new people.

Prize bonds.

Who knew?

Who the fuck knew?

A staple of my father's generation, they bought them for their family's future. The Lotto and lotteries of every ilk came down the greed pike and these forgotten bonds languished in drawers or between the pages of family Bibles never opened.

I had, due to a threat on my father's reputation, rummaged among his few possessions.

Kept in a Lyons tea chest, his few papers scorched my heart. A certificate of loyalty to the Knights of Columbanus, an inter-counties semifinal medal in hurling, now as tarnished as the country. A faded picture of *the family* at — get this — the fucking beach.

Not exactly a Californian scene. Didn't evoke a Beach Boys theme.

No.

My parents in their street clothes, with a summer concession of my father's — sleeves rolled up. My mother was wearing what might have then been called a summer frock.

Save they didn't do *seasonal*.

She wore the same item in winter, with a cardigan added. Always her one habitual trait, the bitterness, leaking from her down-turned mouth to every resentful fibre of her being.

I was maybe eight in the photo, an ugly child who grew to embrace ugliness as a birthright.

Tellingly, my father's hands were on my shoulders, my mother's folded in that "What are you looking at?" pose she perfected every day of her miserable life.

My mother wasn't a simple bitch.

She was more evolved, a cunning sociopath who hated the world under the guise of piety.

Dead for years now.

Did I finally, Oprah-like, come to understand?

Yes, alleluia.

Forgive?

Like fuck.

And, oh my God, she would spin in her grave to know those prize bonds were sitting there. There may not be justice, but there sure is some cosmic twisted karma. Took a while for the bonds to be processed, but when they were, I was stunned.

Cash.

Lots of it.

So I stopped drinking.

How weird is that? When I couldn't afford it on any level, I went at it like a famished greyhound. Now, I quit?

Go figure.

Three months in, I was doing OK, not gasping, hanging in there and feeling a whole lot healthier. I'd been down this road so many times, but something had altered. My last case, I literally lost two fingers, and witnessed some events that shadowed me in a new way. I finally figured out booze wasn't easing my torture but fine-tuning it. Would it last? Who knew?

I was sitting in Garavan's, just off Shop Street. It still resembled the old pubs: an Irish barman, snug, no bouncers, decent slow-pulled pints and memories of the bearable kind. Pat, a middle-aged guy, was tending the pumps, brought me a black coffee, a glass of sparkling water. He was off the booze his own self, so no jibes, said,

"I'm off the cigs."

He was old-school smoker, mainlined nicotine. I said the usual hollow things, ended with,

"Did you use the patches?"

"Fear," he said.

Whether of health, economics or his wife, I didn't push.

Life needs a touch of mystery and not everything requires an answer.

2

"Some people, I saw, had drowned right away. And some people were drowning in slow motion, drowning a little bit at a time, and would be drowning for years. And some people, like Mick, had always been drowning. They just didn't know what to call it until now."

Sara Gran, *City of the Dead*

"Purgatory is the pit stop en route to hell."

KB

The woman sat opposite me, didn't ask, just sat. This used to happen a lot. People believing I had some inside track for finding things — people, solutions, maybe answers. I'd found some answers over the years and they were always the wrong ones. Or right, but for the wrong reasons. I'd given it up with the booze, the cigs, the Xanax.

Before she could speak, I said,

"No."

Knocked her back.

Her mouth made a small O of surprise. I knew the gig.

The touching photo.

Some heart-kicking story.

Her son/daughter/husband

missing,

was a great/caring/lovable

individual,

and

could I find them, what happened to them?

The whole usual awful parade of misery.

She tried,

"But they said you care."

I said,
"I don't."
And I didn't.
Not no more.
Sorry.

My new home was a steal.
Literally.
Galway, in the boom years, was the most sought-after location for housing in the country. Plus the most expensive. Now with the new austerity, the bankruptcy, you couldn't give away property. I rented a two-bedroom, ground-floor, bright, open apartment in Merchants Road, not a spit from the Garda station.

Flat-screen TV, modern kitchen for all the cooking I'd never do. Large pine bookcase. I'd given Vinny a shout at Charlie Byrne's bookshop and he'd stacked the shelves. He knew my books, sometimes even knew me. Plus, he'd handed me an envelope, said,
"It was left in the shop for you."
No, he hadn't seen who dropped it off.
My name on a deep-blue envelope, almost the colour of a Guard's tunic. Inside a photo of a young man on a skateboard, high in the air, looking like an eagle against the sky. Then a piece from the *Galway Advertiser* which read:

. . . verdict due on 10 January in vicious rape case.
Tim Rourke, accused of the brutal rape and battery of two young girls, is due in court for the verdict. Controversy has surrounded the case since

16

it was revealed that the Guards had not followed procedure regarding the evidence.

There was more, about this being the latest high-profile case likely to be thrown out on some technicality. And still
the bankers,
developers,
clergy,
continued to fuck us over every way they could.
A single piece of notepaper had this printed on it

Jack, you want to take this one? Your turn.
   C33.

3

"*Right, she thought, I'm just having a little attack of metaphysics.*"

Fred Vargas, *The Chalk Circle Man*

"*Philosophy is for the man of private means.*"

Oscar Wilde

Stewart was more a reluctant ally than a friend. A former yuppie dope-dealer, he'd been sent to jail for six years, hard full sentence. I'd solved the murder of his sister; he'd felt an enduring debt since. From his release, he'd reinvented himself as a Zen-spouting entrepreneur. And seemed to make shitloads of cash. Even in the depths of the current bleak economy. We'd been thrown together on numerous cases and he'd developed a strong friendship with my other ally.

Ridge.

Sergeant Ní Iomaire.

A gay Guard, married to a bollix. She was currently out of the marriage but moving up the ranks, slowly in the all-male hierarchy of the police. They seemed to believe I was redeemable.

Not yet.

Stewart was sitting in the lobby of the Meryck Hotel. It fed his posh aspirations and served herbal tea. A crime in any venue. Wearing an Armani suit, he sat at ease, like a cat with breeding. I was drinking black coffee, bitter as my heart. I showed him the note, article, photo I'd received. He gave his full focus. Said,

"Let me check on this photo. It looks familiar."

Then he read aloud the message, which was
Your turn, Jack.
Looked at me, asked,
"What do you figure?"
I told the truth.
"No idea."
He pushed.
"And?"
"And . . . nothing. I don't care."
He let out a small sigh, stole a glance at my mutilated
hand. I wore a glove, gave the appearance of having all
the fingers. He pushed his tea aside, made a gesture
with his head.
Annoyance?
Asked,
"Why are you showing it to me, then?"
"You see, Stewart, you have the tendency to want to
know the answer to . . . Jesus, everything. I thought this
might keep you off the streets."
He didn't rise to the bait, asked,
"If I work it out, am I to tell you, to *report back?*"
I said,
"Tell Ridge. She might give a fuck."
He scanned the note again, asked,
"C33?"
And before I could take a shot, he said,
"Right, you don't give a toss."
I was moving away fast, despite my limp — acting up
less these days — when Stewart shouted,
"What about that dude Reardon?"
Let him shout.

Bí cúramach!
Indeed.

The Reardon Riddle?

Talk of the town. One of the rarities, a dotcom billionaire who'd survived the current global meltdown, had come to Galway, set up headquarters and, according to rumour, was going to save the city. Not yet forty, the guy was allegedly a blend of Steve Jobs, Gandhi and Putin. Didn't hurt that he looked more like a roadie than a star, gave that *edge* vibe.

When priests had to disguise their clerical collars due to public ire, it helped that this whizz kid didn't look like the other loathed species, bankers.

His trademark jeans and trainers were more Armani than Penney's, but hey, who was judging?

Was he too good to be true?

We were about to find out. But the buzz was all good thus far. I mean, fuck, he'd even said he'd like to save Galway United. On the smart board, this was cute twice over.

When I was a child, the nearest family we had to royalty were the Hunters. They made prams — I shit thee not — but had the Anglo-Irish gig down. Owned a large — get this — white mansion, at the rear of Galway. They were steady employers, reputed to be *decent folk*, i.e., they'd actually greet a person, if sparingly.

Like our economy, belief, decency, they were in the wind.

Reardon had bought their old home and extensive renovations were underway.

See, employment right there.

I'd watched a rare interview he'd given. Long, tangled, "Dude, just got out of the shower" hair.

The aforementioned jeans and a sweatshirt that was just faded enough to read,

Pogues Rule.

This guy had his shit down.

He'd given one of those rambling monologues, ablaze with sound bites, signifying nothing. But he had a way of doling out this crap, you could believe it made some sense. His accent was a hybrid of surfer dude, Michael Flatley-style Irish brogue, geek.

Somewhere in this mess, he'd been asked about his single status.

He winked . . . fucking winked, went coy about *hoping* to meet an Irish girl. That's when I threw up.

Ridge phoned me as I was reading about the former hangman, Pierrepoint. The State had released papers previously sealed from the public and all sorts of weird, startling data were flooding the news. Pierrepoint had offered to hang two people with the deal,

"Ten pound for the first and I'll do the nephew for half price."

Jesus.

The forerunner of all those offers,

Buy one, get one free.

Ridge asked,

"Am I interrupting something?"

"Tales of the hangman."

A pause.

The question hovered,

"Are you drinking?"

But it passed and she asked,

"Will you help me out?"

Uh-oh.

As they say in literary novels,

No good would come of it.

Ridge had married Anthony Hemple, an upper-class Anglo-Irish bollix. He wanted a mother for his daughter, she wanted juice for promotion to sergeant. They were now separated. I said,

"Well, sergeant, spit it out."

"I've been invited to a party. I want to go, but I need a partner."

I let her stew, then,

"How come you didn't ask Stewart?"

"He's already going with a young lady."

"What's the occasion?"

"The Reardon party."

The party.

Reardon had altered the Hunter house to accommodate his reputation, down to a helipad on the extended roof. The setting remained spectacular, not one other property nearby and the golf links spreading out to reveal the whole of Galway Bay. It made even the bloody rain look attractive. I was dressed in my one suit, the funeral job. Black and from a charity shop. I was suffering a panic attack, no Jay, no X, no cigs, thinking,

"Am I out of me fooking mind?"

I was loath to attend public events as just recently a newspaper, in lieu of anything new or out of sheer bollock laziness, re-hashed the story of, as they headlined it,

The Tragedy of Serena May.

Replayed all those terrible events. My closest friends, Jeff and Cathy, had a daughter with Down's Syndrome. The light of their lives and mine. I adored that child, spent many hours as the bedraggled excuse for a babysitter. Until, Jesus, a terrible accident and the child was killed. Years later I was exonerated of blame, but the mud stuck. The thinking was,

"Taylor was there."

And true, as the Americans say, it happened on my watch.

The article didn't scream,

"Taylor did it."

But published a furtive photo of me and you thought,

"The fucker did something."

All it took.

Suggestion.

Ridge asked,

"You all right, Jack?"

Given that I'd never, in me whole bedraggled, befuddled existence, been *all right*, I had to bite down on the sarcasm, always bubbling under, then,

"Yeah, not using anything, it's a trip. Like Richard Ferrara. I've been down so long, maybe it will seem like up."

Being Ridge, she asked the wrong question.

"And Richard Ferrara, how did he fare?"

I could have been tactful, lied, but I don't do nice, not ever, said,

"O.D."

Shut that baby right down.

The Hunter place was ablaze with light, like a beacon of false hope to the city. As we got out of the car, Ridge handing over the keys to a parking guy, she said,

"'Tis rumoured the Saw Doctors might show, play their number-one hit, with Petula Clark's 'Downtown'."

Now that would seem like up.

The best and the brightest were not at the party.

They'd emigrated.

What we had were the shoddy and the smiles. The Galway celebrities, who'd yet to make it to *The Late Late Show* but claimed they'd got the call. Waiters in livery, I kid you not, were dispensing champagne. Ridge took a glass and the waiter, familiar in a bad way, said to me,

"It's free, Taylor."

I said,

"It's a lot of things, but free ain't one of them."

I heard him mutter,

"Kent."

And no, he didn't think I was from the county.

Stewart approached, a dark girl in tow, looking like Beyoncé in her younger days. He had, as the Brits say, an *impeccable* evening suit and what appeared to be a maroon cummerbund.

Jesus wept.

He introduced her as

"Tiffany."

Of course, no chance we'd be running into too many named Mary. Out of absolute zero interest, I asked,

"And do you work . . . um . . .?"

Couldn't quite bring myself to utter the name. She gave a champagne giggle, said,

"How droll."

I've been called every variety of bollix, but this was a first. She countered,

"And you, John, do you?"

Great.

"It's Jack. I insult people."

She was game, went with it.

"And does it keep you?"

"Off the streets, at least."

Stewart whisked her away, fast. Ridge glared at me, but a man was coming up on her right, dressed in ratty jeans, battered Converse and a sweatshirt with the logo

I'm a gas.

Yeah.

Reardon.

He hugged Ridge, said,

"Sergeant Ní Iomaire, great to see you."

Then turned to me.

Ridge said,

"Jack Taylor."

He didn't take my extended hand and it hung there, like a government promise, sad and empty. His eyes were dark brown, close to black, with a curious light at the corner, as if he'd had them highlighted. The guy had presence, no denying that, but a pity he was the one most impressed by its glow. He asked,

"You the guy who got the handicapped kid killed?"

Tim Rourke was born nasty, got worse. He'd been in trouble all his life, liked trouble. Liked to *hurt* people. He should have just been lost in a lost system, but the social workers discovered him. The workers with *awareness*.

The ones who *cared*, in italics.

Julie Nesbit, in particular. All of twenty-six years of age, with accreditation from London. And determined to make her mark. Rourke charmed her. A serial rapist with a dirty soul, he'd managed to con her into the belief that if only someone would believe in him, ah, he'd be gold.

Like that.

She had that rare ability, given mostly to judges and priests, to completely ignore all the evidence. They didn't think outside the box, they were fucking buried in it. A measure of Rourke's psycho charm, borne out by Nesbit's description of this spawn of Satan as

"*a cheeky monkey*".

Her impassioned plea before the judge, in what the Guards had believed was a slam dunk, turned the verdict. Rourke walked — rather strutted — free.

Was he grateful?

Yeah.

Nesbit, rushing to him on the courtroom steps, expecting a wave of gratitude, got,

"Fuck off, cunt."

4

"She can be delicately morbid."

Alice Blanchard, *The Breathtaker*

"Purgatory is seen as hell light."

KB

Rourke should have been a good-looking kid. Tousled blond hair like a character in a chick-lit novel, delicate build, but the eyes . . . the eyes contained an essence that had come from a place of eternal dread. They conveyed the black energy that drove on hate. He never wondered why he had more of this emotion than all others; he learned early to conceal it, to use a knife-like charm to evade responsibility, and derived almost ecstatic bliss from the inflicting of pain.

His type does well in
the army
and
the Church.

Now, late on a Friday night, thrown out of a pub on the Quays, he'd ended up near Nimmo's Pier. He'd trolled here before, robbing gays, penny ante dope-dealers. He'd been downing the working stiff's cocaine, vodka and Red Bull, not that Rourke and work had ever met. His acquittal was blurred in his mind due to the amount of booze he'd taken, and a hit of the new solvent doing the rounds added an extra level of confusion to his head.

All he felt was the usual compulsion to wreak damage. He moved to the end of the pier and looked up at the lone light hanging above the rim. The bulb was gone so he was in virtual darkness. Saw the figure weaving towards him and his body went into attack mode. Then a moment of confusion.

Was the figure moving very fast and . . . moving in a direct line *towards* him?

WTF?

Then he thought,

"Good, come to Momma."

Then a hand was reaching out and he felt the full voltage of the taser. His brain briefly registered,

Born to be wild.

I was on a female mystery kick, reading only lady crime-writers. My contribution to equality. Had asked Vinny to stack my new bookshelves with them.

He did.

I skimmed through the authors:

Sara Gran,

Zoë Sharp,

Margaret Murphy,

Wendy Hornsby,

Lynn S. Hightower,

Megan Abbott,

Cornelia Read,

Alafair Burke,

Hilary Davidson,

Jan Burke,

and was content.

A further two boxes were yet to be opened and I kept the anticipation of that for the dire days of February. The radio was tuned to Jimmy Norman and he was playing the new album from Marc Roberts. You could think that most was OK in my narrow world. Apart from a desperate yearning to get hammered, but I knew how those demons roared. Could see clearly in my mind

the double Jameson,

two tabs of Xanax,

pack of Major.

Almost in sync, I scratched the patch on my left arm, muttered Not today. Was reaching for a book when my mobile shrilled.

Stewart. Said,

"Need to talk to you urgently."

"Thought you Zen masters didn't do . . . you know . . . urgency."

He sighed, then,

"Jack, it's serious — about the note you received."

We met in Crowes bar in Bohermore. My choice. A sign in the window declared,

Bohermore's first mayor.

Michael Crowe, one of the brothers who owned the bar, was indeed the mayor and a good one. Stewart was from a middle-class family, reared in Devon Park, which in my day said,

"You're posh."

Not really, but the notion still lingered. Meant that Stewart didn't know the family and Stewart made it his business to know almost all the players. I was sitting at the bar, groaning at a sparkling water, discussing hurling with Ollie Crowe, when Stewart arrived. In yet another fantastic suit. Coming in the swing door, he brought the sun with him.

Ollie muttered,

"Hell of a suit."

Moved off.

After the usual fandango about Stewart's bloody herbal tea, we moved to a table. Stewart had a serious expression, laid out the clippings I'd given him, the note. Said,

"Take another look."

"Why? I remember the damn thing and C33, or whatever the fooking number is."

He leaned on the notes, so I reached over, took them. Made a show of concentrated interest.

Stewart took a genteel sip of the tea, then said,

"Rourke, the guy due in court?"

I said,

"Sounds like a nasty piece of work."

"Not any more."

"Why?"

"Apparent suicide, from the lone lamp-post on Nimmo's Pier."

"Apparent?"

"I had a chat with Ridge."

I sneered, bile leaking over my tone.

"And ye concluded what?"

"He'd been tasered first."

I digested this, mulled over a few ideas. Pls are renowned for *mulling*. I said,

"Either way, the bad bastard is no loss. Good riddance."

Stewart never quite came to terms with what he saw as my cold heart. If he only knew the half of it. He asked,

"What about the note, the phrase *Your turn?*"

I had a longing for a short, sharp jolt of Jameson, so intense I could taste it. Tried to shuck it away, said,

"Another eejit, the city is full of them. Some of them are even running it."

Stewart had that light in his eyes meant he'd done some digging, gone that extra mile. He said,

"The skateboarder who was shot? He was dealing dope."

I took a shot.

"*You* dealt dope."

He took the hit, not well, but ran with it, said,

"This guy dealt to school kids."

I finally got it, did a double take, asked,

"You think somebody took out . . . killed . . . those *wrongdoers?*"

Made a mental note to seriously stop thinking in italics. Added the dreaded word, in mocking fashion,

"Vigilante?"

He stayed the course, said,

"Worse."

Surprised me, and before I could speak, he added,

"And I think he wants you to play."

5

"*He looked at her again, at the white body by the black water, surrounded by dark spruce trees. The scene had nothing of violence in it. In fact, it looked peaceful.*"

Karin Fossum, *Don't Look Back*

"*I've never seen much good press on Purgatory.*"

Galway nun

Sister Maeve gave nuns a good name. My history with her had started real fine. Even went for cappuccino and croissants, relished her joy at such a rare treat. Then, par for my course, things hit the shitter, bad and ugly, and she deleted me from her life. Few can freeze you like the clergy, and the nuns learn early in nun school how to deliver that withering look.

I'm stunned, a compliment almost!

Then, busting a rib in the Devil, she came to me for help with a delicate case of missing funds, and I came through. I wasn't back on her prayer list, but neither was she watching the papers for my obituary.

I was in Java, the designer coffee shop, when she found me. I didn't recognize her at first as she was in civilian clobber. And thank fook I didn't burst with,

"Didn't know you without your habit."

She said,

"Jack."

Her smile was hesitant, but still had that radiance leaking at the corner of her mouth. A cupid's bow that Ridge said "was fecking wasted on a nun".

Maybe.

I said,

"Sister, good to see you."

I offered a seat and she demurely took it. Nuns, if this isn't too weird, have a trait in common with French women.

Delicacy.

A grace of movement, economical but compelling. I asked,

"Cappuccino? And they have cheesecake fresh out of the bakery."

She was thrilled. I mean you've got to love a person who is so easily fulfilled. Buckets of Jameson, acres of Virginia leaf, a whole mess of pharmaceuticals, lines of pints, and I was as near to peace as the Church to the people.

Her fare came and she set to with gusto. It was a pleasure to see her demolish that cheesecake. I asked,

"Another?"

"Oh, I couldn't."

But no heart in it.

I said,

"A little wickedness gives us all something for the confessional."

I settled back in my chair and she gave me that nun appraisal, all encompassing. I came up short, I already knew that. But I had credit in the ecclesiastical bank, so I waited. She said,

"You look well, Mr Taylor."

No point in trying,

"Jack."

So I went with,

"Thank you."

But this wasn't a social call, the get-together-with-the-local-thug gig. She said,

"I find, or we . . . the Church . . . are in need of your valuable assistance once more."

I bit down on sarcasm too easy and I figured, take a run at a nun, all kinds of shite coming down the karma pike. I said,

"If I can."

She produced a sheet of paper, laid it on the table, asked,

"Are you familiar with 'Our Lady of Galway'?"

Knock,

Lourdes,

Medjugorje,

sure.

But Galway?

Really?

Not that it would hurt the tourist trade. Always money in devotion, and if you can find the Madonna on a wall, bingo. Work it.

I said,

"No."

This is the short version.

Our Lady of Galway.

A seventeenth-century Italian statue of Our Lady. She holds a stunning mother-of-pearl rosary in her hand, donated by a Claddagh fisherman. The first Catholic mayor of Galway, in 1683, put a gold crown on the head of the statue.

The Penal Laws came down the pike, Catholics were forbidden to practise. The statue was buried by a man named Brown who, after the persecution was over, presented it to the Dominican order.

They resided in an old thatched church in the Claddagh. A new church was erected in 1891. The Madonna, the centrepiece of the church, has an altar showing

a Claddagh fishing boat,

St Edna, the patron saint of the Claddagh,

and

St Nicholas, saint of Galway.

A week previously, someone nicked the statue.

Thus Sister Maeve.

She said,

"Of course, we don't expect you to work for free."

They did.

This was just cover-your-arse nicety.

I played.

"No need for that."

Did she argue?

Guess.

Peg Ramsay was not a nice lady. There was little in her back-ground to indicate she'd become a mean, vicious, greedy cow. She was simply a bad bitch. Her husband had been a money-lender, on a small scale, without too much intimidation in tow. Junk food, brandy took him out in his early fifties. Peg decided to up the game.

Recruited two East Europeans who learned their trade in the Serbo-Croat conflict.

Learned to be vicious.
Francis
and
Xavier
Known collectively as FX.
Their special effect was to break all the bones in the
face. All the bones.
Slowly.
The face has a surprising number of bones.
And there were a not-so-surprising number of
debtors.
Peg had a few ground rules. Never to be wavered
from.
The amount.
Three grand.
Lent for a month.
You wanted less?
Fuck off.
But people in need, who'd turn down the extra
euros?
The vig?
That was purely on a whim. Depending how bitter
Peg was feeling on a due day. She worked on the
maxim,
"Ground them."
I was looking at a poorly shot photo of Peg. FX
could be faintly glimpsed in the background. Stewart
had come to my apartment in a state of agitation,
pushing the above picture at me, and an envelope. I
snapped,

"And what happened to *Hello, how are you?* And maybe, *Hey, nice place.* You know, like *manners?*"

I'd been up late, watching the Super Bowl, watching the New York Giants win for the second time in four years, watching Madonna strut her stuff, and I was tired, cranky. Watching sport without a six pack seemed *wrong!*

I was on my first coffee, and not feeling the kick. I asked,

"Who's this?"

He was in no mood for bollix, said,

"See this fucking envelope? My name is on this. Why am I being dragged into this shite?"

Phew-oh.

Stewart and cursing were rarely in the same room, let alone sentence. His Zen seemed to have taken a holiday. I looked at the photo, then took the envelope, pulled out a sheet of paper, read,

. . . Stewart, Jack seems reluctant to play, so . . .
This is Peg Ramsay. Want to take this one and maybe we can get
Jack on board?
C33

Stewart had, of course, checked out Peg and told me who she was. I asked the obvious.

"Is she still with us?"

Got the look. I said,

"Hey, come on, it's a relevant question."

He shook his head, said,

"You know what we have to do?"
I said,
"Not a clue. The Guards?"
"We have to warn her."
My turn to gasp; asked,
"Are you fucking kidding?"

6

"The Burning of Auchindoun"

Traditional folk song, sung by Sophie Ramsay

Stewart had a new BMW. I shit thee not. This kid was pulling down some serious change. With the rest of the country in the economic toilet, he was buying a new motor?

I asked him,

"How do you do it?"

Changing gear, as we veered off from the main drag of Eyre Square, heading down to the docks, to Long Walk, opposite the Claddagh, he went,

"Huh?"

He knew. I said,

"The new car?"

"Perk of the job."

Fucking with me. Then to divert me, asked,

"The party, what happened there, you and Reardon not going to be best buds?"

Jesus.

I snarled,

"Stop talking like you're off the set of *The Kardashians*."

Got him.

We were coming up on the Spanish Arch, the Thai restaurant to our right. He spluttered,

"You're familiar with the . . . *The Kardashians?*"

Hard not to be, like a virus there was no stopping. I went with,

"I left early because parties without a Jameson are like Zen without the echoing yawn."

Cheap shot but you take what you can.

Told him how as I was walking down Threadneedle Road a limo had pulled up. Yeah, an actual limo, and a woman in her thirties offered me

a ride home.

In the American sense. She was, she said, Kelly, *Mr Reardon's* PR director. It was starting to rain so I took the lift, and kind of liked Kelly. A displaced New Yorker, she had that Louis CK sense of humour, so what's not to like?

And she was an avid reader of Anglo-Irish literature. Oscar Wilde being, she added,

"her doctoral subject".

Only Americans can quite get this reverence when talking about books. An Irish person would say,

"Read Wilde; not bad."

Stewart was sliding the car close to the water on Long Walk. He asked,

"You like her?"

"We're having coffee in a few days."

He wanted more but we were right outside Peg Ramsay's office. No one could accuse her of false advertising. A large sign declared,

Loans.

Stewart said,

"Take it easy, OK?"

"Hey, your idea to come. I'm saying fuck all."

A no-frills office, with a plain wooden desk, four hard chairs and FX.

Francis and Xavier.

The Serbians, in dark suits, looking like the book ends of a very bad novel. Their faces carried expressions of hard, uncompromising dullness. They had the appearance of being related by malignity. The only difference I could see was one wore a tie.

The tieless one strutted over, growled,

"Yes?"

Stewart said,

"We'd like to see Mrs Ramsay."

The guy could care fucking less, asked,

"Why?"

"Personal business."

He'd been looking at Stewart like he wanted to eat him, turned a lazy eye on me, said,

"Ring, make appointment."

I said,

"Hey, deliver the message. Keep the hard-arse act for someone who gives a shit."

He was surprised, then gave a tiny smile. I saw him flex his body, then he took a breath, let it slide.

Peg was a heft of a lady, in her rough fifties, with a face that no make-up was ever going to conceal, a face that had learned hard. A shit load of jewellery that rankled like a conscience when she moved. A smoker's pallor, that colour I know, inside and out. She rasped,

"Taylor, well I'll be fucked."

Nice.

I asked,

"We met?"

She made a T sign to one of the Serbs, then said to me,

"In my business it pays to know the high-profile drunks."

She let her eyes slide over to Stewart, said,

"The Nancy I don't know."

Stewart had done six hard years in Mountjoy. Name-calling wasn't high on his radar. He asked,

"Would you believe we came here to warn you?"

The returning Serb, tea on a tray, moved a little faster on the word *warn*; the tieless one was already in place, behind Stewart. Realizing, Stewart said,

"We have some stuff here that seems to indicate you might be in danger."

The tea plus chocolate biscuits were in front of Peg, and Stewart placed the photos, the threat before her. She took a healthy bite of chocolate, noisily said, mouth full,

"This a shakedown?"

Sounding like a really poor dame noire, she seemed only vaguely interested. I jumped in, said,

"Sorry to have taken up your time."

Moved to leave. Tieless stepped in front of me, growled,

"You no go."

Peg asked,

"You want me to believe you came here out of . . . Jesus . . . good citizenship?"

Stewart said,

"At least you can be on guard."

Peg did the most unexpected thing of all: she smiled.

"*Garsún*, I'm on guard 24/7."

This got a snort from the Serbs.

I stared at the tieless Serb for a moment, he stepped aside.

We moved to leave and Peg shouted,

"You run into financial difficulties, you remember your Aunt Peg."

Outside, I said,

"The sooner the bitch gets strung up, the better."

Stewart shook his head, said,

"I thought she had, you know, a shine for you."

No answer to that. I looked across at the Claddagh church, asked,

"You ever hear of Our Lady of Galway?"

He thought, then,

"Circa 1780?"

I nearly punched him, said,

"Nobody likes a fucking show-off."

I began the task of finding Our Lady. The irony was not lost on me. A recovering Catholic, mired in guilt, remorse — is there any other kind? — seeking the mother of God.

There was one essential to finding her.

Faith.

Kidding.

Money.

Yes.

So I began the round of pubs, churches, dives, flop houses, derelict buildings, student accommodation, crazies, neo-pagan sub-cults, nuns, all the band of would-be Madonna theft. Spreading, if not the joy, at least the cash.

And found her!

Swear to Jesus.

Lost her as fast.

A miracle in its wicked self. Minty, a street guy who favoured, get this, crème de menthe, above all — thus his name — was the new go-to guy on my information street. For years it had been Caz, a slick Romanian who'd become my uneasy friend.

And got killed.

Not directly because of my friendship, but in there.

Like that.

Minty had come to me, offering street cred, rumours, the half-truth that existed on any Galway street in times of deep hardship. Rumour faking as fact, like the government. It's the Irish way. Least it was now. I'd get Minty some bottles of that awful liqueur and he'd tell me mostly what I wanted to hear. There was always that kernel of truth hidden but I had to sift.

Curious and also never able to mind my own damn business, I'd asked why that drink, got,

"It's a class thing. You really wouldn't understand."

I found him on the steps of the Augustinian church, just before eleven a.m. Mass let out. It was, he said,

"Good takings to kick the day off."

I told him what I was looking for. He was dressed for combat in a long Irish army coat, Doc Martens, and seemed more student than bum. He was of that indeterminate street age, beat, worn, wary. Could be a bad thirty, or sixty. I palmed him some euros, said,

"I'll get you some of the de menthe later."

He nodded, said,

"Jack, it's getting rougher out here."

I knew.

I waited, then got,

"Young hoody, name of Brennan, he took the statue, stashed it in his old man's garage, somewhere in Newcastle. The kid plays at being *street* but he's just a spoiled bollix, taking a holy statue would seem to him to be . . . *edgy.*"

Minty threw his eyes up at this nonsense.

Case solved.

I asked,

"How do you know this stuff?"

He shrugged, no biggie, said,

"It's an art, but not great."

Before he went fucking deep on me, I asked,

"And Brennan might be, where?"

"Down at the swamp. He and his mates smoke shit down there."

I said,

"The Church thanks you."

He shuddered, protested.

"Don't be fucking putting no jinx on me. Jesus."

I found the young guy where Minty said.

And we'd a song and dance as he did tough in front of his mates, strutted until I gave him a sharp cuff on the ear. Does wonders, that.

Short, sharp, educational.

Brennan had the face McNeice described.

"Low cunning."

But, yes, yes, he'd taken the statue, for

"the craic".

And yes, it was in his father's garage. I said,

"Let's go get it."

The kid was barely eighteen, but attitude and stupidity were fighting for supremacy. He asked,

"What's in it for me?"

The day had started well. I didn't want to spoil it with beating the be-Jaysus out of this eejit. I said,

"The Church has, I'll agree, lost a lot of its clout, but, still, the local hard guys go to Mass of a Sunday. How d'you think those hurlers would treat a pipsqueak who stole Our Lady?"

He'd deliver it outside the Claddagh church at noon the next day.

In time for the Angelus.

I know, dammit, I should have gone right then, but I was complacent. It had been too easy. My history told me,

"I don't do easy."

The next day, Brennan was there, without the statue. He'd imbibed something to make him a whole new deal, said,

"We've moved the statue to a new place."

Jesus.

I eyeballed him, asked,

"Not the church, I'm guessing."

His faint smirk now blossomed, he said,

"Ten large by Saturday or the dame goes in the river."

"The dame!"

I was so surprised, I did nothing and he strutted off. I'd have admired him for his sheer brass if it didn't piss me off so much. I did something I thought I'd never do.

I called the Guards.

Ridge met me in the GBC, one of the few remaining Galway cafés not only surviving but thriving. They kept it real simple. Good food and cheap. Ridge was in plain clothes, a promotion since the last case we'd been on. Dressed in a new navy tracksuit, white stripes, she looked healthy, less intense. Few could simmer like her. She said,

"Word is you're still off everything: cigs, dope, booze."

I gave her my second-best smile, no relation to warmth. She said,

"After the party, you know, what Reardon said, I thought, you know . . ."

I knew.

I told her about the statue, gave her Brennan's name, said,

"You were to visit now, I think the statue would still be there."

She stared at me, then,

"Why are you not doing this your own self?"

Told the truth.

"I'm getting old and makes you look good with the Church."

She smiled and I actually felt good.

Forgetting smiles are a prelude to nothing good.

Ever.

She said,

"I've been watching the video of *The Bodyguard* all weekend."

Whitney Houston had been found dead in the Beverly Hills Hilton. I wondered if Ridge's interest had been fuelled by the gay innuendo that had followed Houston. I was too cute to ask, cute in the Irish sense of sly hoor.

I nodded sagely, as if I understood.

I didn't.

How do you blow a hundred million?

Ben Gazzara died the same week and no fanfare. Ridge said,

"That clip, she sings 'I Will Always Love You' and pauses. You know, her lip quivers, she's going for the high note and nails it."

I went,

"Hmm."

But Ridge was going philosophical.

"Whitney never hit that note again."

I said,

"Apropos of nothing, some of us never hit that note."

Got,

as she stood to leave,

"Some of us just never got the right song."

★   ★   ★

I'd recently come across *The Psychopath Test* as compiled by the FBI. Jon Ronson had written a book of that title. I'd been compiling my own variation, the AT, as in

The Asshole Test.

I was pretty sure that anyone who used

apropos

made the list.

Late that evening, before she clocked off work, Ridge decided to call on the garage, the one holding the statue. Knocking at the main house, she got no reply, then walked round to the garage. She was hit from behind with some form of iron bar, left in a heap on the ground. Either then, or in the next few minutes, her Claddagh ring was torn from her finger, her watch, twenty euros and her warrant card were all taken.

I didn't hear until next morning, Stewart shouting into my mobile,

"Why don't you answer your fucking phone?"

I said,

"I had an early night."

He was fighting for air, control, spat,

"Yeah? While you were sleeping, Ridge was being wheeled into ICU."

Jesus.

That was all the detail. I asked,

"Where?"

Heard with a sinking heart the address I'd given her.

Stewart picked up on my tone, accused,

"You know something about this. Ah, no, you sent her on one of your fucking jobs."

My silence was assent.

He said,

"You bollix, you're a . . . a . . . plague."

Rang off.

I didn't go on the piss.

I went ballistic.

7

A Mind of Winter

Shira Nayman

My hurley was almost bent from previous outings. Made by a man in Prospect Hill, he still used the ash: cut, polished and honed the wood to a sheen and, if asked, would add the metal rings around the end of the stick for traction.

Kidding about the traction.

Since the loss of the fingers on my right hand, I'd become adept at compensating; had wound a tight leather strap on the handle of the hurley. It had been a while since last I'd employed the stick. Ridge, then horrified at the use I'd put it to, had made me swear never to use it again.

I swore.

Swearing is easy.

I placed it in a sports bag that proclaimed,

Mervue United.

Shucked into my all-weather Garda coat, item 1834, that the Department of Justice continued to try to repossess. From habit, I reached for the staples: the Xanax, a lethal shot of Jay, a pack of cigs.

Nope.

Going to dance this reel with plain old-fashioned rage, bile and bitterness.

Fuel of a whole other hue.

I checked my breathing: level, not what you'd expect for a guy with murder in his soul. I slung the bag over my shoulder, headed out. Ran into a man I used to know in my cop days. He'd been a player, became one of those predators they called *speculators*; had him, he told me once, a portfolio of quarter of a billion.

On paper.

And with Anglo-Irish.

As wiped and gone now as the promise of poverty eradication.

I thought then what I thought now on his losses.

Fuck 'em.

He stopped, peered at my sports bag, asked,

"Going to the gym?"

Of course gyms, saunas would have been part of his tycoon's life, then. I said,

"Well, a workout, sort of."

He said,

"So sad about Eamonn Deacy."

Our most cherished local sporting hero; what Messi was to Barcelona, he was to Galway.

Made me pause. When we didn't have heroes any more, just poisonous celebrities, Eamonn was the quiet, unassuming figure that a hero was meant to be. The man before me shuffled, looked to his left, so a touch was imminent. He said,

"Heard you were doing good."

Not health or emotional well-being, no.

Cash.

I said,

"Getting by."

He gave a bitter laugh, went,

"Fuck, in these days, that is doing brilliant."

I reached for a note, saw it was a fifty.

Mm-mm.

Bit large for a street encounter — few of them and I'd be street me own self. I palmed it over as discreetly as these things can be. He stared at it. Yeah, hadn't figured on me for that largesse.

Wrong.

"The fuck is this?"

Not gratitude then. I began to move off, tempted to get the hurley out. He shouted,

"Last of the big fucking spenders, eh, Taylor? Don't let it break the bloody bank."

You give a few notes to a guy on the street, you're hardly going to go back, kick the living crap out of him, take the money back, but Jesus, it was tempting.

Brennan's house was on the side road that runs parallel to Snipe Avenue, Newcastle. A line of five majestic homes, built from Connemara granite, built to last. With large front gardens and signs that proclaimed,

No accommodation.

Translate that:

Students, fuck off.

In the heartland of the university. Balls, if nought else. St Martins, name on the house. I readjusted the bag on my shoulder, ready to unleash the hurley. I felt the mix of adrenaline fused with rage as I moved up to the front door. In the next garden, a little girl was

standing, staring at me. Dressed in dungarees, with
a flow of red hair, she looked like an urchin from a
Dickens stage adaptation or a refugee from the
abominable *Annie*.

Before I rang the doorbell, she said,

"Nobody home."

I stepped back, trying to rein in the rush I was
feeling, asked,

"Yeah?"

Her face, freckled like a Spielberg extra, minus the
bike, squeezed up. She said,

"*Yeah* is very impolite."

The fuck?

She stepped closer to where I was standing. I was
very conscious of . . . an old guy talking to a young girl.

Jesus.

Lynch mobs would meet for a whisper. Her accent
was upper middle class; that is,

posh,

moneyed,

condescending.

She said,

"You are probably the new poor."

What?

I asked,

"Are you on medication?"

She said,

"I'm nearly a teenager."

Good to know. I asked,

"You didn't by any chance see the Virgin Mary?"

Realizing how daft that sounded, though in Ireland we did have a history of moving statues, as if the Mother of God was on tour. She duly scoffed, said,

"Hardly, I'm a Protestant."

Accounted for the accent and probably the attitude. She asked,

"Do you have a business card?"

I let the exasperation leak on my words, said,

"What would you do with a business card?"

She sighed, said,

"Pretty obvious you never heard of LinkedIn."

I made to push off and she asked,

"Your name, sir?"

Christ, she'd make a great cop.

I wasn't sure of the etiquette of formally meeting teenagers. Do you go,

"Yo"?

And, like, high five?

I said,

"Jack Taylor."

She mulled that over, then gave,

"I'm Dell."

"What, like the comics?"

Exasperated her.

"Don't be silly, Jacques, it's from Odell."

Truth to tell, she made me veer between incredulity and laughter. I echoed,

"Jacques, seriously?"

And got a look of such withering contempt takes most people half a lifetime to learn. She nigh spit,

"One tried to give you some class refinement, Mr Taylor."

Seeing as I'd made the trip, was here, I asked,

"You didn't see what happened to the Ban Garda, the female police officer, yesterday?"

"Hardly. One doesn't snoop on one's neighbours."

Whatever the fuck that meant. I said,

"OK, see you then."

As if it just struck her, she asked,

"Have you been very old for a very long time?"

Did cross my mind that I might find a use for the hurley after all.

I didn't ring Brennan's door as a strong instinct urged me not to.

I was walking down the Newcastle Road, students to the left of me, winos to the right.

A Blue Datsun pulled up, almost on the kerb, a burly ape emerged, and I thought,

Guards.

In a bad suit but with the thick-soled shoes you never forget — matches the crust of the spirit — the guy stonewalled me. I knew him. We were almost related by beatings. Usually him doling them out. Named Lee, he gave bullying the X factor. Worked at it, constantly.

"Get in the car," he rasped.

Smoker's voice, waylaid by second-rate whiskey. The bell for the Angelus rang from the cathedral and no one seemed to bless themselves but me.

I asked, staring at the car,

"Not buying Irish, then?"

Got bundled into the car, my holdall thrown with me. The driver glanced at the hurley, muttered,

"A concealed weapon."

Lee said,

"Super needs a word."

Clancy.

My one-time close friend, we were brother Guards on the force until I got bounced and he got promoted all the way. Recently, he'd been honoured by the university: Honorary Doctorate, flash dinner, photo on the front page of the *Galway Advertiser*, all the glittering prizes. We'd clashed many times over the befuddled years, his loathing of me growing in proportion to my defects.

At Mill Street, I was marched before him in his new spacious office, a riot of photo opportunity, mostly golf shots of him with the rich and crooked. The odd bishop to add colour if not dignity to the montage. He was in full uniform, a large oak desk with orderly files at his left. I said,

"Dr Clancy."

Lee was behind me, barely restrained.

Clancy looked up, distaste writ huge, said,

"Always the smart mouth, Taylor."

Before I could summon up something *smart*, he added,

"So, they cut off your fingers a time ago."

Indeed.

Lee said,

"Pity it wasn't his balls."

Clancy indicated the holdall, the hurley, said,

"Should be good for six months."

I said,

"Not to mention good PR. Guards bust man for love of the national sport."

Clancy got to his feet, shoulders back, pot belly well concealed beneath expensive tailoring, but there. He said,

"Sergeant Ní Iomaire was hurt in an incident. The wrath of Jesus will descend on you if your name comes up in the investigation."

Not the time to mention Ridge was seeking . . . the Virgin Mary. Christ, it would sound like a deranged spiritual odyssey. I could have brought up the weird photos, C33, but he'd just ridicule it. He rasped,

"Get out of my sight."

They confiscated the holdall, bad bastards. Outside, I nearly reached for a cigarette, did the deep-breath gig instead. Turned towards the hospital, frustration dancing with anger in my daily reel of reproach. I bought the paper, the shop guy asking,

"Cigs, Jack?"

I said no and he ventured,

"Rolling your own, eh?"

No answer to that.

Athens was burning anew as the Greeks faced further medieval measures to offset the massive bailout. Dire predictions on every financial front and still, get this, the banks' directors awarded themselves massive bonuses.

No wonder the Virgin Mary was MIA.

The Artist won five Oscars. Some deep message in the fact that a silent movie was top of the heap but I was fucked if I knew it.

Ridge was still in critical care. Stewart was pacing the corridor, he snapped at me,

"Didn't break your neck getting here."

I let that slide, asked what the doctor said.

The next forty hours would be critical.

I said,

"I'm going to try and track down Brennan. If he attacked Ridge, he better hope I don't find him."

Stewart said,

"You and C33 make a fine team."

8

"You'd lose a farm in one bet, take you twenty years to drink it."

Old Irish saying

Peg Ramsay thought no more of Jack Taylor, his bizarre account of some lunatic maybe posing a threat. She'd laughed.

Jesus wept. She had more enemies than the Church had excuses.

She stood in the foyer of her new home. A magnificent seven-bedroom house, built in the boom by a property whizz who was now in jail. She'd bought it for a quarter of the asking price, the market being now more a turkey shoot than a business. Her minders/collectors, FX, were four rooms away, chowing down in the vast kitchen. Rottweilers, she thought, loyal as long as she fed them.

She climbed the wide ornate stairway to the third floor, muttered,

"Third floor! Phew, count 'em and weep, yah bad bastards."

Pride in her achievements gave her a rush, a sheer jolt of energy that propelled her up the stairs. She stopped, leaned on the balustrade and wondered,

"Maybe some paintings along the walls?"

Buy a shitload of art. Like everything in the country, artists were on sale. She registered a sound a split

second before the arm went round her throat, the knee
in her back. Then a hand on her spine and she thought,
Over the balustrade?
A voice whispered,

"My heart is as some famine-murdered land
whence all good things have perished utterly
And well I know my soul in hell must lie."

One:
her body halfway over the rail.
Two:
a deep effort of breath.
Push,
and fly,
the foyer rushing to smash her startled face.
A DIY petrol bomb landed on her back and with a
whoosh illuminated the marble inlay.

9

"He always liked laundromats. They're like waiting rooms for people who never travel."

Sorry, Zoran Drvenkar

"Purgatory was deceptive in its promise, that you might one day be released."

KB

The American woman who'd given me a lift home from Reardon's party phoned to confirm our coffee date. We arranged to meet in Griffin's Bakery café, but you had to get there early, before the lunchtime gang. I made an effort, wore a white shirt, ironed, 501s and my Garda-issue coat. Trying for that blend of

I tried I don't give a fuck.

Checked the mirror, thought mainly I looked old. But good, real good, to be meeting with a woman. Jesus, I'd nearly forgotten how that felt. So OK, some negatives:

1. She worked for Reardon.
2. See above.

The little time I'd spent that evening with her, I liked her. She was smart, caustic, and I seemed to amuse her in a vague fashion. Her age seemed to hover in that blurred could-be-thirty, probably-forty set.

She was waiting outside when I arrived, said,

"You're sober!"

Registered my face, went,

"Kidding, sorry. Jeez, Jack, these are the jokes, right?"

I nearly turned on my heel, but took a deep breath, ushered her in. A long line of people at the counter for the Grinder — the speciality bread that had a taste like wish fulfilment. We got a table close to the wall, and I got a good look at Kelly.

But, oh fuck.

Skinny jeans.

Jesus weeping. And in that puke mustard shade that seemed to be the only damn colour they were flogging. The hell was with that? OK, she was thin, that voguish starved-with-a-tan look.

Skinny jeans. I wanted to roar,

"No,

  No,

    Never."

Unless you are a teenager or the bass player with Kasabian.

She ordered soda bread, Galtee cheese, Barry's tea. Said,

"Get all my carbs stashed."

No sane answer to that. I ordered a double espresso. She said,

"Bitter, huh?"

Our fare arrived and she laid on the thick Kerrygold butter with gusto, said,

"Reardon, my boss, he has . . . more than a passing interest in you."

"Why?"

She was on her second round of bread. Jesus, this girl could eat, washed it down with tea, burped without fanfare, said,

82

"His research into the town, its recent history . . . your name keeps coming up, be it the swans, the tinkers, the Church, Magdalene laundries, and you are, he feels, *a person of interest*."

I thought about this, then said,

"I feel he has plans for the city."

She whistled, low but definite, said,

"Oh, yeah, like you wouldn't believe, and, who knows, maybe a part for you."

I gave her my rabid smile, let that be its own reply. I drained the last of my coffee and, sure enough, down the yearning pike came the nicotine blues. She looked at me, asked,

"How long since you smoked?"

She was good.

I said,

"Well, I was the kind of dedicated smoker who smoked between cigarettes."

She quoted,

" 'A cigarette is the perfect type of perfect pleasure. It is exquisite and it leaves one unsatisfied.' "

I hazarded,

"Simon Gray, *The Smoking Diaries*."

I could tell that went over her gorgeous head. She said,

"*The Picture of Dorian Gray*."

I ordered more coffee, got some palpitations running. She asked,

"Top of your head, no thinking, favourite book?"

"*The Book Thief*."

Surprised her.

Fuck, surprised me.
She asked,
"You ever married?"
"No."
She gave a radiant smile, then,
"Me neither. What's your excuse?"
Tell the truth, then it's their gig, said,
"Drink."
She considered that. I asked,
"You?"
No hesitation.
"Never met anyone like my dad."
Was she kidding?
Her mobile shrilled. She checked it, said,
"The mighty Reardon calls."
Outside, we had that awkward moment,
do you mumble some vague shite about staying in touch?
Go,
That was nice, let's never do it again.
She asked,
"Want to see me another time?"
I asked,
"Do I remind you of your father?"
She was moving, stopped, said,
"Don't be ridiculous, he is a good man."

10

"*Draw a picture of my soul and it'd be a scribble with fangs.*"

Gillian Flynn, *Dark Places*

"*Souls in Purgatory are supposed to be on day release.*"

KB

I was arranging my DVDs on a shelf, mug of coffee in my hand, cigarette on my mind.

Stepped back, looked.

Game of Thrones, Series Two,

Breaking Bad, Series Four,

Treme,

Weeds, the whole seven seasons,

Conspiracy: The Wannsee Conference, the Final Solution,

Damages, Series Four, with John Goodman.

You put John Goodman in a series, I'm there.

On the coffee table, strewn almost casually, was *Matter of Heart: The Extraordinary Journey of Jung into the Soul*.

Visitors would be impressed. The empty walls sneered,

What visitors?

A heavy book, and I'm talking actual weight,

Gitta Sereny, *Albert Speer: His Battle with Truth*.

I intended to give this to Stewart, all eight hundred pages of fine, tight print.

And speak of the Devil, my mobile rang.

He said,

"The statue was found in the canal."

Took me a moment to catch up. I snapped,

"No hello? You know, the Zen niceties?"

He was ready.

"The sarcasm, Jack, it gets old, like you. Ridge is still in a coma; how's that for fucking nice?"

Rang off.

Shook my head. His language was way down the shitter now.

St Laurence O'Toole, the patron saint of Dublin, whose heart was preserved since the twelfth century.

I know, sounds like the Irish *Twilight Zone*.

Thieves figured the heart had to be covered in gold, right?

And stole it.

Around the country, small churches were reporting the theft of chalices, gold crosses. A priest exclaimed,

"Have they no respect?"

Where the fuck had he been for the past decade?

Our Lady of Galway had been spotted by a dog walker, submerged among the litter of a hen party at the Dominic Street end of the canal. The Brennans were still lying low, but I fully intended having

a wee chat.

I rang Sister Maeve, who despite my protests seemed to think I had a part in the statue being found. She promised,

"The Church will not forget you."

Sounded faintly like a velvet threat.

I was heading down Shop Street, the weather in early-spring mode, mime artists and buskers on the streets, a guy flogging time-shares in Greece, proclaiming,

"Buy now while the Greeks are broke."

Like Saint Laurence, there was little gold in his heart.

Reardon had finally shown up in person at my apartment, insisting he treat me to dinner. He was dressed in chic grunge — scuffed trainers, hoodie, combats — but oddly, these emphasized that he was older than I'd figured. Deep black splotches under his eyes testified to either work, insomnia, dope or all three.

I was surprised when I opened the door to see him, muttered,

"What?"

"We need to talk."

Before I could ask,

"About the fuck what?"

he glanced at his watch. Yeah, a heavy gold Rolex job and no knock-off, too fake-looking to be false. Like the Pope.

He said,

"The Arch, new joint in Kirwan's Lane, do biblical steaks they tell me."

What the hell, see if I could get a handle on the guy. Grabbed my Garda-issue jacket and he said,

"Ah, the infamous government one."

I said what I thought.

"It's downright creepy how much you know about me."

He laughed, one of those nurtured on Marlboro Red and Wild Turkey, so I kind of liked him a bit better.

It was a short walk to the lane, buskers doing everything from

"Galway Girl"

to

The Undertones.

Mainly massacring any tune you ever liked.

He'd a table booked. I had noticed two heavy guys a discreet distance behind. He said,

"My guys."

"You need security."

As we were seated at what I figured to be a table for eleven, he went,

"Guy has as much green as I do, two ain't even enough."

Ain't.

Pronounced with a Midwest emphasized twang. Irony or just pig ignorance?

Waiters surrounded us like altar boys feeding a bishop. I asked,

"You intending to buy Galway?"

He scanned the menu, nodded.

"Pretty much."

The wine waiter presented a bottle of some antique vintage. Reardon snapped,

"Bring two pints of Guinness, Jameson back."

I said,

"I'm not drinking."

He smiled. I saw the inner steel, a glimpse of the blaze that made mega bucks. He said,

"Tonight you are."

I did.

As I sipped the head of the pint, my heart hammering, I asked,

"What next — lines of . . .?"

"Not before the dessert."

Fair enough.

We had steaks, his blood raw, mine medium, circled by mashed spuds, blitzed with gravy. Least mine were; he went the ketchup gig. He ate with a restrained ferocity, as if he loathed the food but, by Christ, he'd get the better of it.

Like that.

I overheard the table next to us, stopped mid-fork, focused.

They were talking about the killing of the money-lender. *In her own house!*

Reardon asked,

"You OK?"

I snapped,

"Gimme your phone."

iPhone, naturally, did everything save the ironing. Got through to Stewart, asked,

"You heard?"

"You mean Peg Ramsay?"

"It's true, then?"

I could hear his despair, anger, then,

"Yeah, in her own home, thrown from the top of the stairs."

Christ, tried to get my head around this, asked,

"And FX, the so-called bodyguards, where the fuck were they?"

Reardon watched me with lazy interest, a small smile dancing near the corner of his eyes.

Stewart said,

"In the kitchen."

"You are fucking kidding. What? Making tea? Jesus."

He waited, then,

"We have to do something, right?"

Yeah, sure.

Said,

"Any change in Ridge?"

"No."

Rang off.

Reardon took his phone back, looked at the number, noting it, saving it, said,

"I don't do friends."

Maybe it was Peg Ramsay, maybe the pint of Guinness. I went,

"Just what exactly led you to believe I give a flying fuck?"

Stopped him. Then,

"Dude, you really are the wrath."

Pushing his plate aside, he ventured,

"You interest me. You're a sort of Irish Zelig, witness to the history of Galway.

The Magdalene,

the swans,

the tinkers,

despair of the young generation,

clerical abuse."

Paused, drank a fair whack of Guinness, continued,

"See, I figure guy like that sees trends, and maybe can keep me up to speed on certain elements."

The prospect of just one, swear to God, Jameson, lightened me. I said,

"Paid tout."

He shrugged.

"Whatever."

Could work. Least I could take his money. That would definitely work. He paid the bill with a platinum card, impressing the shite out of the waiters, me, half of Quay Street.

We're shallow, so sue us.

Outside, I offered,

"Nightcap?"

He sighed, said,

"Told you about friends."

I near shouted,

"Lighten up. It's a drink, not a fucking commitment."

We went to the Quays, ghosts of drinks past, bitter and recriminatory. A few guys sitting at the bar nodded, not in a friendly fashion, more the

We *see you*

Irish warmth with cunning outrider.

We had us some shots of Jameson. Reardon holding the shot to the light, saying,

"See why it is you do this shit."

He didn't.

I said,

"No, you don't."

He wasn't bothered, lazily asked,

"You get on with anyone?"

I shucked into my jacket, said,

"Been fun but, you know, enough."

He walked out with me, palmed me a phial, said,

"You got five pills there. Ease that hangover right easy tomorrow but, like my job offer, it's a one-shot deal."

I said,

"As opposed to One Direction."

We were standing in Quay Street, crowds of people swarming in the constant search for the *craic*, Irish party time. Involved gallons of drink, some blow, and who knows, that evasive, all-encompassing, fulfilling moment. No sign of the brutal economic austerity. Drinks on the *Titanic* indeed. Reardon's mobile shrilled again. He moved into Kirwans Lane to take it. I moved with him but with enough space for privacy. And saw,

top of the lane, Ma.

The Feebs.

First, I thought it was an urban illusion, the booze, the rush of Quay Street, but, no, here they were, myth on foot. Five teenagers, green T-shirts with the Feeb logo.

FBI.

Fucked

Boozing

Irish.

The logo on the green T-shirts now being sported by a new phenomenon: a gang of feral, vicious teenagers who specialized in urban mayhem, inner-city terrorism. The courts seemed reluctant to send them to the young offenders' units, due to the lack of money available for staff. Knowing this, The Feebs were growing bolder.

Looking indeed feral, up for it. Three guys, two girls, the guys holding bottles of cider and wine spritzers. Moving with intent.

To us.

I nudged Reardon, who, engrossed in his call, waved me off. The gang moved closer, one of the girls making sucking noises. They spread out; bad idea. I pulled Reardon's arm, snapped,

"Pressing matters!"

He looked up and, I swear, smiled. Grasping the drift instantly.

First guy said,

"Hey, fuckheads."

Reardon laughed, said,

"Love it."

And he was moving. Took out the first guy with a kick, moved to the second, a chop.

Down.

The third, two rapid slaps.

Then to the girls, said,

"Ladies."

Moved.

Lashed with his open hand the ears of both, swung round, sunk his trainer in the arse of the first, looked at me, asked,

"Want some?"

Five hangover pills. A cure is a blessed reprieve but a loaded gun, too.

Next morning, the hangover phoned it in.

The pills kicked ass. I vaguely remembered hitting some late-night clubs and, oh fuck, scoring some dodgy coke off an even dodgier dopehead. Getting home, I was wired and drunk, bad combo, watched TV.

I kid thee not, a documentary on teenage pyjama girls. That went viral. The two girls featured wear pyjamas, in and out, all day,

smoke forty fags,

use the C-word incessantly,

drink strong cider,

search for drugs,

and were both

fourteen years old.

In deep shit at school,

no job prospects,

Worked at being *hard*, as in

"Hey, c***, what'cha looking at? Want yer head kicked in?"

And yet, maybe it was the Jameson, they seemed to possess a sweetness that they fought like little bees to hide.

This was Ireland's youth.

And I do recall wanting to weep.

Oh.

And swearing off the drink.

Stewart had always tried to rein in the worst excesses of Jack's temper. Jack was so . . . *extreme*. Truly believed that the courts gave out the law, and alleys dispensed justice. He favoured the latter, with a hurley. Over the years, Stewart had been part of some horrendous violence, but never, Jesus, God forbid, gratuitous, and, fuck no, never got a kick out of it. He was beginning to suspect, albeit reluctantly, that there was a part of Jack that relished acting outside the law.

And, whisper it,

liked the rush.

He'd seen the light, a dullness become radiant, as Jack lashed into some thug. More, he seemed now to seek out the cases where it would end in a purity of blood-letting.

With Zen, his martial arts iron training, stepped up, Stewart was literally trying to purge his own self of the charisma of violence. The dark thrill of control, meting out punishment. But the last twenty-four hours had shaken him. He loved Ridge.

No question.

They'd shared a house on the last case, seen the horrors up close and personal, and together shared the bond of futile attempts to redeem Jack. Only Stewart's feelings for his dead sister even came close to the elusive love he swore he didn't need. Prison had scorched granite into his being, had had to, to survive. He found that same shell vital as an entrepreneur.

Dragon's Den?

He rented them the fucking den.

Sources, the fuel of information, were key. Lots of minor characters, like in a novel, chorusing the narrative, spurring the impetus, never less than essential. Bit players in the clubs, pubs, streets of Galway.

And, oh, they loved to talk.

Tell a story.

Any story.

And sometimes, the truth was in there, just a wee bit tangled. As in the late call to his mobile last night. The voice saying,

"Brennan, father of the brat who stole the statue of Our Lady, he's the one who fucked up Ridge."

Click.

The line went dead. Google search. Brennan, a beaut. Thug city in a suit.

If a good one, Louis Copeland no less.

Brennan had come quietly from Dublin, smartly avoiding the round-up of the original psycho drug-dealers:

the General,

John Gilligan,

the Monk,

and had kept under the radar as those larger-than-life scumbags went national, prompting

movies,

TV documentaries,

countless tabloid fodder.

With the creation of CAB, the special unit to nail those guys on their illegal assets, Brennan had fled to the west, gradually seeping into the Galway geography like vile limestone. His only son, the statue stealer, was a grave disappointment to the would-be Irish drug lord. Built an empire of dirt and dope, and had an eejit heir.

Seemed karma right.

Brennan, in his sixties, was still a formidable physical presence and, like Jack, favoured a hurley for his ad hoc boardroom meetings. Rumoured to have recently taken out a rival dealer with two mighty wallops to the guy's head, shouting,

"Come on the Dubs."

Didn't make him any more appealing, despite his support of the capital's team. In the few available photos from Google, he looked like Gérard Depardieu without the Gallic charm. An eye for the ladies, was said to be proud of his *fuck pad*. A penthouse over the Bridge Mills. What his wife thought was not recorded. But going on Brennan's reputed temper, she wasn't likely to be saying a whole bunch.

Beating women seemed to be a hobby. Ridge, asking questions, especially about his worthless son, would have been an automatic trigger.

Stewart had three tasks Zen-appropriated this day.

His sister,

the *Galway Advertiser*,

Brennan.

Did the second by phone. Rang, asked for Kernan Andrews, said,

"Kernan, am leaving a batch of photos, notes about a number of recent Galway deaths in the office for you."

Heard,

"What?"

Hung up.

Next, went to Going Dutch, the best florist in the city, bought a dozen white roses.

Walked to the Bohermore cemetery.

A huge monument to a young tinker was visible from the road. Locals wondered how the mega tribute, adorned in Connemara marble, could be affordable to the travellers. At night, it was fluorescent, sending a beacon of dazzling light across the nearby hill. Had converted many a heavy drinker who believed they'd had a portent direct from the Lord Himself.

To reach his sister's resting place, he had to walk by a long line of young men who'd committed suicide in the previous few years. Their families had laid
football sweaters,
football boots,
CDs,
little fluffy toys,
intricate scrolled tablets of love,
making the graves more like the boys' bedrooms than graves. It appalled and moved Stewart in equal measure. He reached his sister, stood, the tears threatening, bent, tidied the loose clay. A passing old woman paused, offered,
"Sorry for your trouble."
He muttered,
"Thank you."
Not with too much warmth, though he appreciated the words. This was his sister's time. Needed to visit in quiet. Sensing something, she asked,
"Your wife?"
"My sister."
The woman stared at the stone, saw the dates, then said,
"Ah, sure, the bed of heaven, *a leanbh*."
That pierced his heart anew.

11

"Galway: an irony-free zone?"

Stewart

Stewart stood outside the Bridge Mills, lots of people around. A voice in his head telling him,

Leave it alone, this is not the way to get Brennan.
Weighed that.
Moved.
He was in the penthouse in five minutes, the burglar kit making entrance easy. He'd taken the precaution of wearing surgical gloves. The place was massive, testament to a guy with too much money and no taste. Gigantic TV, copies of

Autos,
Penthouse,
Hustler,
Loaded.
Ikea furniture, a heavy cloud of blended weed, nicotine, curries and empty pizza boxes. The bedroom had a walk-in closet, four Louis Copeland suits, twenty pairs of built-up shoes, tracksuits and a set of weights. Under the mattress, a sawn-off shotgun, bags of coke. Enough to warrant a major bust. Stewart moved back to the front room, settled to wait.

He let his mind Zen float, his body at ease, time suspended.

The apartment was dark when he heard keys in the front door. Didn't move.

Brennan came storming in, lights going on, packages being strewn on the floor. He was making a drink near the window when he realized he wasn't alone. Spun round, going

"The fuck?"

Stewart continued to sit, stared at him. Brennan was dressed in a sweaty tracksuit, gym clothes, a white towel round his neck. Stewart stood, did a loosening exercise, asked,

"Why did you attack Ridge?"

Brennan was regaining his composure, his eyes darting to the bedroom, assessing how much of a threat there was. His expression answered,

Not much.

He said,

"Sonny, you picked the wrong fucking place to park your sorry arse."

When Stewart didn't answer, he pushed,

"And who the fuck is Ridge?"

Stewart said,

"A female Guard, asking about your dumb son stealing the statue."

Brennan laughed.

A nasty blend of scorn and bile.

He asked,

"You're not a cop? Was she your girlfriend? I got to tell you, fellah, she was one ugly cunt."

All reservations, doubts about the value of violence, moral considerations vanished with the mention of the

C-word. Stewart shot out his left foot, catching Brennan in the crotch, followed through with a series of lightning kicks to the ribs, kidneys, face.

Finally, drawing breath, he pulled back, looked almost in wonder at the bundle at his feet, muttered,

"Jesus."

Checked for a pulse. Faint. Got outside the penthouse, left the door open and called an ambulance. Back on the street, he looked in dismay at his hands, the gloves coated in red, understood maybe for the first time why Jack needed a large Jameson after an event.

He dumped the bloody gloves in the trash.

Zen didn't quite cut it.

12

*"The household tax is to Ireland what the poll tax
was to the UK. The beginning of bullying."*

Galway protester

Ridge woke up.

Her head hurt and she emitted a tiny groan. A nurse came, did the pillow-fluffing. No matter what state you were in, those fucking pillows had to be fluffed.

A lot.

The nurse asked,

"How are you?"

Took Ridge a moment to figure.

"Who am I?"

Then pieces of it surfaced: knocking on Brennan's door, anticipating verbal aggression but not an onslaught. After the first blow, she was blank. Put her hands to her face. She asked the nurse bringing some water,

"Am I . . . damaged?"

Irish nurses, their very directness is refreshing. She said,

"Ah, you took a fierce hiding."

Right.

Added,

"But you're awake, that's good."

Argue that.

The doctor came, did some hmm-ing, said,

"Nothing serious, really."

Unless you counted a coma.

She asked,

"Was I out for long?"

"Yes. Trust me, you'd prefer not to know."

Then,

"A day, two, you'll be going home."

Ridge, relieved, said,

"Good as new."

The nurse gave her a look, translated as,

"Don't be bloody stupid."

Yuppie, in dump café: "Do you perchance have Wifi access?"

Owner: "I don't have bloody access to me kids."

I was sitting in Elaine's, the newest coffee shop off Shop Street. Kelly was sitting opposite, on her second macchiato. She'd been asking me about my hearing aid, then moved on to the loss of my fingers, said,

"Not enough of you left to even mail, fellah."

I was developing a deep affection for her. She had a mouth on her, kept my game up, and she was that rarity,

interesting.

I mean, in a world of Lindsay Lohans, who is interesting any more? Romney was fast-tracking towards the Republican nomination, Barack was simply looking tired, and the brief dark glitz of Newt was dissipated. I said,

"I had a night out with Reardon."

She laughed, went,

"Whoa, now that I would have paid serious wedge to witness."

I debated, then,

"We ran into a spot of bother."

And she literally guffawed, echoed,

"A spot of bother. What are you, a freaking Brit suddenly?"

Ignoring that,

"A gang of wannabe tried to take us out."

Her eyes were lit. She said,

"Right up Reardon's block. He likes to get down and dirty."

Her glee set off an alarm.

I asked,

"You mean, Jesus Christ, he fucking staged it?"

She was saved from replying by a large man who, without asking, sat at our table, glared at me. Kelly went,

"Seriously?"

He produced a wallet, his plain clothes ID, said,

"Thought you might prefer an informal chat rather than the barracks again."

Jesus, did anyone still call the cop station that?

I asked,

"You have a name?"

He showed some very expensive bridgework, allowed,

"Foley."

I waited.

"Where were you yesterday, late afternoon?"

Kelly said,

"He was with me."

I wasn't.

Foley gave her a look of utter disbelief, said,

"And you are . . ."

Now she smiled, took a sip of her coffee, went,

"I'm what's known in the trade as an *alibi*, presuming you wouldn't be asking if something hadn't happened."

He looked like walloping her wouldn't be too much of a reach, said,

"You need to be very sure, Miss, of what you're telling me."

She was delighted, cooed,

"I love it! You are so rigidly . . . *anal*."

I asked,

"What happened?"

Like he was going to tell me. He stood up, turned to Kelly, warned,

"You're a Yank, a visitor to our shores. Be in your interest not to . . ."

He paused.

His big moment.

"Not to *fuck* with the authorities."

She gave a mock shiver, said,

"Show me your weapon, Foley."

After he'd left, I said,

"Watch your back. Those guys, they remember."

She signalled for the bill, said,

"My treat."

Added,

"Those guys, you can see them. It's the motherfuckers who hide in plain sight I worry about."

I had no idea what this meant but it sounded hard core.

Thanked her for the coffee and she said,

"What do I get in return?"

I had my own question, asked,

"Why did you lie for me? You weren't with me."

And she gave me the gift of a full warm-to-warmest smile, said,

"Yeah, but you're thinking, *wish she was*."

Not far off the truth.

She said,

"Invite me to your apartment."

"What, now?"

She sighed.

"Jesus, Jack. Get real, buddy. This evening, so you can prepare a meal, get ready to *party*."

Had to know, went,

"Are you fucking with me?"

A kiss on the cheek and,

"That's what you're hoping for later, big boy."

An hour later, unable to get Stewart on the mobile, I found out about Brennan and that Ridge had come round. Bought some flowers and headed for the hospital.

Was I sorry about Brennan?

Yes.

Sorry the fuck wasn't dead.

Laden with white roses, a box of Ferrero Rocher, I arrived in Ridge's room to find Stewart sitting by her bed. He went,

"What kept you?"

I ignored him, put the stuff down, moved to Ridge. Her face was covered in those yellow-blue marks that are a sign of healing. You can only surmise from their ferocity how bad the beating was. Her eyes were clear but something new in there, a wariness.

Fear?

I hoped to fuck not. A frightened Ridge rose biblical mayhem in my head. I was saved from hugging her by the IV. She smiled, said,

"Tactile as ever, Jack."

I sat on the edge of the bed, feeling like a horse's arse. I said,

"Good news."

Ridge looked like that would be impossible. I added,

"The guy they figured did for you, Brennan — someone paid him a visit."

She sighed.

"Oh, Jack, you didn't?"

True, I had some mileage in this field, but protested.

"I'm guessing it's the C33 lunatic."

Stewart said,

"C33 doesn't leave the victims alive. You'd remember that if you were paying attention."

I swung round, snarled,

"The fuck is the matter with you?"

He waved at Ridge, said,

"I'll be back later, babe."

Strode out.

I was after him, Ridge calling me back.

Caught up with him outside the hospital, a batch of huddled smokers to the right, like the ones God cast out of heaven and as cowed. Stewart gazed at them, muttered,

"Wish I smoked."

I grabbed his shoulder, snapped,

"The fuck is with you?"

He stared me down, but something was amiss with his focus and for a bizarre moment I thought he was stoned.

Stewart!

No way, ever. He'd been a dealer, did his time in jail, he'd eat a bullet before that. But . . .

He said,

"Brennan is at death's door."

I read it wrong and, Jesus, not the first time, asked,

"You think I did it?"

He gave a bitter smile.

"If it was you, Jack, the bastard would be dead, right?"

He moved to go. I asked,

"You're thinking C33, but we didn't get a letter, like the other times."

"Jack, I'm working with all me might to think nothing, nothing at all."

And was gone.

I went back to Ridge and tried to make desultory talk until she exclaimed,

"Jack, you seem out of sorts."

I sighed, sounding horrifically like my despised mother, said,

"Certainly out of something."

13

"*If you don't have sex and you don't do drugs, your rock 'n' roll better be awfully good.*"

Abbie Hoffman

"*Purgatory is what the Americans term a plea deal.*"

KB

Since my evening with Reardon, I'd stayed clear of the booze, but wondered what the tipping point would be for the head-first dive into oblivion. Tried to tell myself I'd done good with the cigs.

"Hey, not smoking, no coke — way to go, fucking St Francis."

I was having the first coffee of the morning, strong, heart-kick gig, using a small hand-exerciser to build up the strength in my right hand, try to compensate for the lost fingers. I'd promised Ridge I'd be there to collect her on her release from the hospital. Her husband was hunting with the local hounds club, I kid thee not, fox-hunting still being permitted on his lands.

His lands.

How utterly fucking Irish is that?

Like the rest of the country, he was in hock to his balls, and yet, the hunt must . . . run.

Fuckers.

The date for the household tax deadline had passed; less than half the population had paid it for the simple reason they couldn't. And now, still reeling from the sheer bullying tactics of this, they were going to introduce water meters in every home. It was like they figured,

"We've broken the spirit of the people, now let's really kick them in the nuts and then fuck them."

Only a short time in power and they already had the distinction of being the most hated government of all time.

Some achievement.

The weather was once again doing its peek-a-boo act, rain to sun to wind to storm and freezing. I wrapped up in my Garda coat, Galway United Scarf, and headed out. A man I'd swear I never saw before fell in step beside me, asking,

"You don't mind if I walk with you, Jack?"

He looked harmless, but what does that mean any more? In his shredded forties, he was short, with a very flash leather jacket, as if he expected a slot on *X-Factor*. I stopped, asked,

"I know you?"

Letting the aggression of no cigs leak over my words. He smiled — good teeth, bad, mean eyes — said,

"Ah, sure, you won't be remembering me, Jack-o."

The faux stage-Irish with the frigging O to my name got to me in ways I'd forgotten. Ways that conjured up the flash of a hurley and steel toe-caps. That is, my days as a Guard.

He said,

"I used to help your Mum. You know, carry the shopping, look after the garden."

My Mum!

Fucksake.

Like she was a slice of Irish whimsy.

She'd been a walking bitch, spat and snarled her way through a sham religiosity, with a tame priest as a buffer. I stopped, asked,

"What did you call her?"

His eyes, startled, went,

What?

My voice cold as yesterday's Mass, I asked,

"Did you call her Ma'am, Mrs, Your ladyship?"

Relief flowed. He said,

"Oh, right, I am . . . Mrs Taylor, you know."

He wasn't even worth a wallop for his worthless lie. I asked,

"And you'll want, how is it? A little something for your *thoughtfulness?*"

He was unsure now, maybe stories of my erratic behaviour had reached him. I shot out my hand, shook his shoulder, said,

"If only we had more of your kind, we'd be a richer country."

And moved past him, a dumbfounded expression on his face.

I got to the hospital, went into the patients' shop, bought some very expensive flowers, a box of flash chocolates and the daily tabloid. The headline screeched about the new sly tax the government was planning.

A water charge.

In Ireland.

Where we were surrounded at every turn by it, now we were to pay for it, with meters to be installed *free of charge*. The woman behind the counter said,

"Now I'll have to give up water, like everything else."

As I came out of the shop, I saw a woman on the edge of my vision and stopped, frozen. The tilt of the head, the way her body moved . . . then saw her face and it was not who I thought.

Time back, I'd been as close to commitment, a relationship, as it ever gets for a loner like me. An American woman, for a few months it was bliss. Made me believe I could feel good about me own self, and that's some leap.

One conversation had leaped into my mind. She'd been listening to my fear of

"It's the dread of becoming boring, that the gold dust will fade, the glitter evaporate."

She'd said,

"Jack, you'll never be boring to me."

I'd snapped,

"Not talking about you."

Outside Ridge's room, I thought about sharing this with her and realized it wouldn't much improve my standing, walked in and found an empty bed. Shock at first, thinking,

Jesus, she's dead.

Until a passing nurse told me she'd checked out last night. We both looked at the array of stuff in my hands. I asked,

"Will you give them to the children's ward?"

She would.

122

★ ★ ★

Back at my apartment, I'd done a fevered job of cleaning, not so easy when one hand is missing digits but I'd learned to compensate. Not smoking, drinking, drugging, I sure had the time, and even, part-time, the energy. Lady Antebellum on the radio, singing about being a little drunk after midnight and needing you now.

Trouble was, I didn't know who I missed the most.

Distracting my own self, I arranged the boxed DVDs for the second time. It gave me a fragile sense of order, of weak control. The titles were a testament to all the shows that had been cancelled after one or two seasons, the ones that didn't cut it.

Eastwards and Down,

The Riches,

Testees,

Bored to Death.

Seemed apt I'd go for shows that didn't last the distance. I phoned Ridge, told her I'd been to the hospital, tried to keep the whine out of my tone. She lashed,

"Oh, *I'm sorry*; should have called you as soon as I got released."

Fuck.

I asked, not so much caring now.

"You doing OK?"

Deep sigh, then,

"Long as I don't have to run any errands for you, I should be fine."

Jesus, the bitterness. I did the only thing you can do, said,

"God bless."

And hung up.

You had to figure: this is how I got on with my friends, imagine the rest of the world. No wonder I drank, the truth being maybe I wasn't drinking half enough. Shook myself. I'd be buried in a bottle in a jig time and I had a meal to prepare. Yup, I was cooking dinner for Kelly. Where did that place our relationship? Dark side of the manic moon.

OK, I could do this.

I'd watched *Come Dine with Me*.

How hard could it be?

Starter.

Fuck, who needs a starter?

Main course.

Could only be Irish stew. You've served your time in the Guards, two things you can do:

use a hurley,

make stew.

Got all the ingredients laid out:

mass of potatoes,

ton of vegetables,

salt,

chorizo.

I kid thee not, chorizo gives it a kick like bargained absolution. Profane but exhilarating. Washing the veg, then slicing, even with my dud hand, was a comfort, as if normality might be accessible, like in a patch. Lashed the lot with the spuds into a huge pot, added a wee dram of the Jay, now leave to cook for a few hours. The smell permeated the apartment like childhood revisited, save we never had the peace such aromas supposedly bring.

I had white wine cooling, Kelly said it was her preference. Made the bed, clean sheets, and ignored what this might imply. Set the table with a red candle centrepiece, then surveyed.

Not bad.

Wanted to call Ridge, describe it, then roar,

"See, I can do this shit."

But she'd say I was drunk. I'd taped the big match, Man City vs. Man U in the game of the decade. Didn't think Kelly would want to watch, but you could dream. I put The Pogues on, sat back as Shane gnarled his way through "Dirty Old Town". Their thirtieth anniversary this year. Who figured Shane would still be around? He made me seem positively teetotal — part of the reason I loved the band.

Now all I had to do was wait.

A tricky gig when I'd oceans of booze right there, but I managed, barely. I'd just checked on the stew, added some more Jay, left it to simmer when the doorbell went off.

"Game on,"

I whispered.

Kelly looked divine, black silk shirt, tight, over white jeans and scuffed boots with a serious heel. Her hair tumbling over her face in that way that begged *wrap your fingers in this*. I said,

"Jeez, you look great."

"I know."

She came in, gave that detailed inspection that women do. Said,

"Zen via poverty."

I laughed, went,

"I'm not that deep."

She plonked herself down on the sofa, said,

"Oh, I know that."

I offered a drink and got,

"Only if you're joining me."

Hmmm . . .

Took that long to reach my decision. As she sipped on a vodka tonic, I drew from a Shiner Bock, checked my stew, sure smelled strong. The slug of Texas beer only increased my nervousness. Second drink in, I suggested we might try the dinner, but no, she produced a spliff, said,

"We mellow out, won't no ways matter how bad the food is."

Fuck.

Trouble was, hitting on the joint made me want a whole pack of Marlboro Red. Must have been strong dope. We're sitting on the floor, piled plates of stew on our laps, eating like munchkins. She said,

"No shit, but this is like being back at Kent State."

Showing I was still in the set, I asked,

"Where you studied?"

"Fuck, no. Where I smoked major dope."

Right.

She asked,

"Am I really flying or do I taste whiskey in this here stew?"

I said,

"That would be crazy."

I cursed my own self. Jesus wept. The mix of dope, food and booze, I felt my eyes droop. Kelly said,

"Hey, Jack, put your head on my shoulder, grab five."

Dammit to hell.

Woke early next morning, blankets round me and no Kelly.

She'd left a note.

"I had my way."

What?

And she'd done the dishes.

To block out my frustration, I switched on the radio.

Sarkozy was gone, Hollande the new president.

You could say he and I got the wake-up call too late.

Quel dommage. Bad fook to it.

14

"An angel in Hell flies in its own little cloud of paradise."

Eckhart

Stewart heard the news late in the evening. He'd been keeping busy, his various business interests, like everything else, leaking money and credibility. Global news was, as usual, dire: Greece about to drop out of the euro; France's new president adding to the unrest; Syria continuing to murder its own people with impunity.

Stewart was restless, his Zen doing little to ease him down, an almost fevered agitation spurring him on. Ridge was due to visit. He'd promised her a meal but had been unable to settle to the preparation. His affection for her was huge, but now all he could think . . .

She's a cop.

How would she respond if he told her of his treatment of Brennan? Beating the guy to an inch of his wretched life. They'd been down a lot of dark roads, but some semblance of justice had been the riding point, even if it didn't warrant close scrutiny. He knew if he'd shared with Jack, how that would go.

"Good riddance to bad rubbish."

Yeah.

The doorbell went. He made a mental leap of control, took a deep breath, opened the door. Ridge, cleaned up, dressed in a black tracksuit, white glowing T-shirt, looked tired: hospital fatigue, shadows under her eyes. She gave him a tight hug and he could feel how thin she was, the years of wear catching up. He lied,

"You look great."

And she laughed.

She sat on the sofa as he prepared tea, being one of the few who appreciated his herbal efforts. She said,

"I miss living here."

A time, last case, he'd given her refuge from her husband and the violence swirling around her. The darkness had reached out, followed them literally to the doorstep, but they'd found a new alliance in each other. To his dismay, he'd enjoyed her company, but one thing he knew, you never travelled back.

Never.

He said,

"It was real good, sister."

Striving not to leak all over the sentiment with his new shadows. Laid out the tea, the soda bread, honey, crackers, her favourite snacks. He sat opposite, willing himself to tell her about Brennan, to share the burden. She said,

"They're advertising for police in Australia."

"What?"

She was serious.

Half the young people were lined up to leave, Australia being very keen to recruit our trained young. Stewart asked,

"But what about Jack?"

She gave a bitter laugh, said,

"We can hardly take him with us."

Us?

She gave him a shy smile, then,

"Couples seem to have a better chance."

He was incredulous, pushed,

"As . . . what?"

"Friends?"

Threw him completely. She moved to pour the tea, reading him wrong, blustered,

"Forget it. It was just a thought. These days, the panic in the air, everybody's desperate."

Sharing with her now was slipping away and it seemed to be more urgent. He started,

"If Jack went after the guy who hurt you, would you . . . you know . . . be angry . . . at the vigilante aspect."

Groaned. The fuck had happened to his facility with language?

She gave a rueful smile, said,

"Thing with Jack, he'd never tell you."

Said like *she admired that.*

They muddled through the tea, both knowing something had changed, but for different reasons each now locked alone, regretting the inability to spew out the truth. She stood and he tried to lighten the mood with,

"Jack in Australia, eh?"

Harsh tone, harsher look. She said,

"Wise up, Stewart."

Added at the door to his silence,

"Jack is fucked, always has been."

★ ★ ★

I was reading about *rinsing*.

Describes young women who post on Twitter, Facebook, that they want, say,

"Diamond earrings, new car, some cash-heavy item."

And an old guy provides.

Seriously.

No physical contact takes place . . . they say.

Jesus, virtual hooking.

The phone rang, heard,

"You like literature, Oscar?"

Kelly.

I went,

"Bit early for it."

Heard the laugh, then,

"See, the thing is, town hall tonight, one night only, 'Irish Literature as Seen Through an Urban Malaise'."

Then she read me the names of the local suspects who'd be discoursing. I said,

"Compelling as that is, tonight is the final part of *The Bridge*."

I explained this Danish-Swedish joint venture, following on the heels of the superb Danish *Borgen*. She sneered,

"Tape it, fellah; why we have the record button."

I protested,

"Trust me, someone would tell me the end. Like when I tape the football, if Chelsea get hammered, some bollix will shout the result across the street."

She said,

"Jesus, and there was me thinking the Syrian situation was a crisis."

I offered,

"We could meet after, grab supper, have our own collaboration, Ireland and US?"

"Heavens to Betsy, Jack, you sound downright decadent."

"*Heavens to Betsy?*"

She laughed again.

"A little down-home folksy for all yah pilgrims."

She rang off.

15

What Dies in Summer

Tom Wright

C33 adored books. Everything about them, would mutter an A — Z of terms, like a mantra.

Thus:

Orihon: A book consisting of a sheet of paper with writing on one side pleated into a concertina fold. From the Japanese art of *Ori*, meaning fold, and *hon*, meaning book. Considered a halfway point between a scroll and a codex (a set of interleaved folios sewn together).

Or a favourite:

Enallage: Meaning "interchange" in Greek. The substitution of a different number for another possibly incorrect one, often for emphasis or effect — like the editorial *we* instead of *I*.

That one in particular had led, indirectly, so to speak, to the adoption of the *nom de plume* C33.

The recent killing of the dog whimperer named Shaw, a former travelling salesman who bred dogs for the designer market and prided himself on being able to reduce any breed to a whimpering mess. C33 kept a special circle of hell for those who abused dogs. It brought out a biblical savagery that seemed appropriate

139

for a beast who tortured canines, the only simply pure gift God had given.

Shaw had been lured to a warehouse off Grattan Road, believing he was buying six Pomeranians, stolen in Belfast.

C33 had chained Shaw as he'd chained dogs, then attached a spiked dog collar, the spikes turning inwards à *la* necklace of thorns. Then taken a baseball bat and proceeded to slowly break every bone in the fucking bastard's body.

Incanting,

"Kenning . . ."

Loud

to

louder,

loudest,

exclaiming in slow measured tones,

"The meaning is, in Old English, a metaphorical phrase."

Paused to wipe sweat off and grab a bottle of — of course — Galway Water, then continued,

"To compound two words that make a new one, in your case."

Laughed hysterically.

Finished with,

"Bone-house."

C33 wondered if maybe this one should be kept off the public radar. C'mon, they'd say,

"To beat someone to death because they mistreated a dog?"

140

Laughed again, watched the light go out of Shaw's eyes, knew they were crazy, whoa, yeah.

The shrinks had laid out that psychopath path in so many ways.

1. Ruthless disregard for others.

C33 laid a hand gently on Shaw's head, said in a Brit accent,

"Surely not?"

2. A truly almost superhuman talent for hiding this from others.

C33 bent down to look into the ruined face of Shaw, shouted,

"Easy? You think it's fucking easy to act like you give a goddamn, good or otherwise?"

What C33 loved, yes, *loved*,

was you never saw a psychopath coming, as they were the most charismatic personalities on the planet.

Giggled.

Couldn't help it, an actual giggle and titter.

"Not to mention their love of dogs."

This did for C33 entirely, who had to sit down, the laughter was so strong, leaning against the battered torso of Shaw, wiping the tears of mirth, for all the world like a couple of good ol' boys whooping it up.

Man and Superman.

16

"He who kills a man kills a reasonable creature; but he who kills a good book kills reason itself."

John Milton

A new referendum on the fiscal treaty looming and the government was using every bullying tactic to cow the voters into the vote they wanted. The Army of Occupation, on Eyre Square, pledged to be unassailable. Four o'clock in the morning, forty Guards swooped and the camp was demolished. They would try and enshrine the date as a new anarchy icon. The Occupiers pledged they'd be back for Phase Two.

The same week, Robin Gibb and Donna Summer died. A DJ termed it *the final death of disco*.

A man was found beaten to death in a warehouse off the Grattan Road. He was, according to neighbours,

"A quiet man with a love of dogs."

Odd the connections the mind makes. I'd been maybe five and my beloved father came home with a pup, a mongrel with every breed included and love being the glue. An only child, I'd been beyond delighted. My mother, who was the she-wolf from the inner sanctum of hell, disguised in a sickly fuzz-buzz religion, asked,

"Another mouth to feed and who is going to find the money?"

A rhetorical question as she'd already known the answer. A week later the dog was gone. She blamed my father, said he'd left the front door open. Years later, in a bad pub in a bad part of town, I'd been told by an elderly tinker,

"Your oul wan, she gave us a pup one time."

I'd finished my pint, said,

"All heart, she was."

He'd blessed himself, said,

"Lord rest her."

Yeah.

I was stopped almost still in the middle of Shop Street by this memory, hated her all over anew. And to add insult to memory, along came the cloud of nicotine posing as a priest, Father Malachy, my nemesis for most of my bedraggled life. My mother's tame escort. Pious widows collected these bitter, soured bachelors passing as priests and spreading bile.

"Taylor,"

he boomed.

Hard to believe but I'd not long ago saved his miserable arse, and was he grateful?

Was he fuck.

A dedicated smoker, he had a cig between cigs and the attendant grey-yellow complexion. His loathing of me bothered me but little any more, though at odd times I relished the chance to rile the bollix.

Malachy reached in his dandruff-flecked jacket, found a crumpled pack of Carroll's, fired up, amid a shocking fit of coughing. To think I missed this addiction. I said,

"Still smoking?"

Got the look and,

"Bastards are saying I can't smoke in me own house."

His face was a picture in held rage. I pushed,

"Bastards. Your house?"

He stared at me like I was thick, said,

"The Church, and the house is me home."

I said,

"I thought the parish owned the house."

He seemed to be on the verge of a coronary, spat,

"Wouldn't be in this state if your mother had done the right thing."

So many things wrong with that sentence, I was almost lost for a reply until I got out,

"My mother? . . . The right thing?"

He was on his next cigarette, though he seemed unaware he was even smoking, said,

"She was supposed to leave me the house."

My astonishment was equalled only by his sheer blindness. I said, very quietly,

"And her *son*, you don't think he had a shout?"

"*You?* You were a thorn in her side. She had to offer you up for the souls in Purgatory."

I was tired of him, his whining, said,

"You have to laugh, though."

"What? You pup, you, what do you mean?"

"She pissed on your bogus piety and your brown-nosing got you the same result as me in the end."

I'd turned to leave. He demanded,

"Result?"

"Yeah . . . fuck all."

Go Fish: How to Win Contempt and Influence People. Political Cartoons by Mr Fish.

Stewart pushed the book aside, just couldn't get his focus right. He tried to ground himself. When one in three families was three months behind in mortgage payments, he should be glad he owned his home. This form of tit-for-tat gratitude never worked for him. Decided he needed to bite down, latch on to something.

C33.

The papers had given it some play but their tone was this wasn't connected, just a series of random psycho acts, and with the country being pulverized by a crazy government, who in truth really gave a fuck if someone was offing *bad guys*?

"Hey, maybe the killer could take a look at the guys running the bloody country?"

Called Jack, arranged a meeting, see what they could shake loose; they'd done it before. Ridge wasn't shaping up to be much help but at least they had a Garda source. His car radio was playing and he caught

"*. . . The Red Hot Chilli Peppers are restoring funk and taking the piss out of wankers who hijacked it and then didn't know what to do with it.*"

Stewart stared at the radio, asked,

"The fuck are you whining on about?"

One thing guaranteed to drive him off his Zen game was *experts* on rock 'n' roll. He turned into Merchants Road, paused, thought,

Not too far from the last killing.

He manoeuvred his car into a space, surprised he'd managed to find a place, was getting out when a tall skinny guy came *galloping*, shouting,

"Hey, you can't park there. Move that car. *Now*."

Stewart took a deep breath, drew on his extensive Zen techniques, asked quietly,

"What?"

Mistake.

Dealing with minor authority, never concede an inch, they'll skin you alive. The guy was dressed in some sort of long yellow coat, like it was a uniform. He looked at Stewart with derision, said,

"Yellow lines, and what do they tell us, eh?"

Stewart summoned the dregs of his dwindling patience, then gave the guy a slap in the mouth, said,

"They should tell us to mind our own freaking business."

Stewart was still rubbing his knuckles when he sat opposite me in Java. I'd ordered him a camomile tea and a double espresso for myself. I asked,

"Hit someone?"

He grinned, said,

"Yeah."

Not sure if he was kidding, I let it slide, said,

"Camomile tea, that's good, right?"

He was different, not in any noticeable way, but the energy, it was now somewhere else, leading him on a whole alternative dance. I asked,

"How is Ridge doing?"

He sipped the tea, his face not showing any love for the beverage, said,

"She's, as you would delicately put it, *fucking off to Australia.*"

His face had taken on a shadow, a blend of anger, sadness and, I don't know, loss? I went,

"But why?"

And now he held my gaze, said,

"You read the papers, watch the news, and you have to ask that?"

I'd finished my coffee without even tasting the bitter bite I relished. The cup was empty and I asked,

"What will we do?"

He gave me a radiant smile, lit with insincerity, said,

"Have to catch C33 before she goes, you think?"

17

"Any library is a good library that does not contain a volume by Jane Austen. Even if it contains no other book."

Mark Twain

C33 fucking hated Jane Austen.

With a ferocity. Even Hollywood was in on the act. How many fucking times and in how many fucking ways could you adapt *Pride and Prejudice?*

Standing in the living room of the next victim, C33 wondered,

Hey, what happened to the fun gig?

The target was what once used to be termed *slum landlord.*

But in Ireland? Believe it, the recession had brought all kinds of nasty shite and this twist was just part of the rabid package. Dolan, an apparently gentle, slightly built landlord, was cleared of intentional killing when one of his houses burned to the ground, taking a mother and two children with it. All fire-safety features were glaringly absent, but during the investigation vital papers were lost. Benefit of the doubt?

Until the second fire and the death of an elderly teacher. And this time blamed the teacher, and a candle! So was Dolan now out of the real-estate biz?

Nope.

But he was about to be retired.

Permanently.

C33 had fixed a gin and tonic, settled in an armchair, might as well get comfortable. Had gone to a lot of grief to find the old model .45. Almost like a Western one. Took the six bullets, which C33 had modified to a DIY hollow point. The barrel spun nicely, almost cinematic and, better, had a resounding click. The drink was sliding down nicely when Dolan arrived home.

A shot just past his left shoulder convinced him this was no joke. C33 asked,

"Any idea why I'm here?"

Dolan, shaken to his core, shook his head and C33 offered,

"Want a drink? Chill?"

No.

C33 waved the gun to the bookshelves, frowned, asked,

"The Jane Austen shit. I mean, seriously?"

Dolan looked round his own room, seeing his bookshelves as if they were a recent addition, muttered,

"You're pointing a gun at me because of my taste in books?"

C33 loved this, might even have felt a pang about having to waste the dude. Said,

"Excuse my misquoting Plath, but . . ."

Paused.

"I kill because it makes me thrill
I kill because it fits."

Laughed.

"Indeed, it does truly make me feel real."

Dolan tried to get a handle on the complete lunatic in his home, wondered if there was a window to do something, heard,

"No, bad idea. I'd shoot you in the gut, belly shot. The torment of the fucking ferociously damned, as the Celts might put it."

Dolan veered, tried,

"That drink?"

C33 was up, displaying an agility, lightness of foot, that showed a vibrant fitness, said,

"Let me do the honours."

Did.

Handed the drink to Dolan, the .45 loosely dangling like the ultimate lethal tease, then, too late, C33 was back in the chair, said,

"Here's the game, fellah."

And in one swift moment raised the barrel of the gun, put it against the right side of the temple,

and pulled the trigger.

Hammer hit on empty, and C33 blew,

"Phew."

Dolan's mind careened from fear through shock to disbelief and he whispered,

"The fuck are you doing?"

C33 smiled, even managed to feign sheepishness, said,

"Thought I might lighten the load and act like you're not the scum you are."

Dolan, again speechless, then tried,

"Scum?"

C33 drained the gin, burped, said,

155

"Whoops, excuse me, where were we? Oh, yeah, you being an arsonist who rents firetraps to those who've no choice, I figured you'd enjoy Russian Roulette, seeing as you've been playing it with your tenants for years, so, in the light of fair play, I went first, and now it's your turn."

Handed over the gun, but Dolan, wary, didn't take it.

C33 made a sad face, said,

"Ah, c'mon, here . . ."

He spun the chamber.

"Now you've an even better . . . shall we say . . . shot?"

Dolan lunged for the gun, grasped it in both hands, levelled it at C33, said,

"You psycho bollix, play this."

Squeezed.

And squeezed.

Nothing.

Nada.

Zilch.

C33 said,

"I lied."

Unity, thought Stewart.

What was the one unifying factor tying the four C33 killings. Had to be something. If they were random, then, fookit. He had converted his living room into, almost, an incident room. And he was thus immersed when Ridge called round. She'd brought old-fashioned lemonade and handmade scones from Griffin's bakery. She also brought a hangover and a book.

Handed it to Stewart.

Days and Nights in Garavan's.

He looked at her face, asked,

"You were on the razz?"

She gave a bleak smile, said,

"If you mean, did I down some vodkas and slimline tonic, then yes."

Then a memory surfaced. She said,

"Oh, and I was talking to the young Garavan heir and he introduced me to Morgan O'Doherty, who wrote said book."

Stewart wanted to roar,

And I give a fuck, why?

Way too close to a Taylor line.

She stared at the walls, lined with names, photos, the four victims accusing her from the frame. She said,

"Either you should have been a Guard or this is, like, seriously creepy."

She swayed, said,

"Shite."

Sunk into a chair, said,

"Forgot to eat."

He couldn't help it, spat,

"You were drinking on an empty stomach?"

Heard the prissiness leaking all over it.

She said,

"Jesus, Mom, sorry, I did have a bag of Tayto, cheese and onion."

He offered,

"I'll make some herbal tea."

She snarled,

"Christ sake, Stew, grow a pair and get me a cure."

Fighting all his instincts, he made her a Seven and Seven, seeing as it was all the booze he had, due to a reference to that drink in an episode of *Sons of Tucson.*

She took a healthy/unhealthy sip, growled,

"Mother of God."

Appreciation or horror, he didn't push. She sat back, said,

"So, what has all this *research* turned up?"

He forgot his pique, sat opposite her, gushed,

"Had to be a connection, right? And I found it."

Waited.

Nothing.

Had to ask,

"Well, don't you have a question?"

She said,

"You wouldn't have a stray cigarette?"

And before he could lose it, added,

"Kidding. Come on, tell me. The thread?"

He wanted to sulk. He was, after all, an Irish male. Conceded,

"Westbury."

Took her a minute, then she asked,

"The lawyer?"

She meant Gerald Westbury, the hotshot famous for defending the foregone guilty. A media star, the camera loved him and he was pretty fond of the lens his own self.

Stewart took a deep breath, said,

"I know it sounds insane, but he's the only one who knew all four. He was their legal counsel and who would be better able to get close to them, know their habits, routines, get right up close?"

Ridge laughed, not any relation to mirth or warmth but something from a time of darkness. She said,

"Well, that's new, instead of defending them he offs them. It's, um . . . a killer closer."

Stewart gathered up a batch of printouts, shoved them at Ridge, said,

"He was brought up in London, excelled at college, could have been King's Inns but married an Irish woman, moved over here, set up as the guy who defends the indefensible."

Ridge's face had regained its colour, albeit a vodka hue. She was animated, said,

"Sounds like the guy should be running for president, not prime suspect."

Stewart delivered his coup, said,

"His wife, yeah? He adored her. She was raped and murdered by persons unknown."

Ridge grimaced, said,

"Jesus, hasn't the poor bastard suffered enough? Now you want to put him in the frame."

The wind went out of Stewart. He'd been so sure she would leap at his theory. He tried,

"You have always gone with my instincts before."

She stood up, said,

"But they were reasoned, possible. This . . . this is just . . . bollix."

The harshness hung between them like a truth that should have kept its head down.

She headed for the door.

No hug.

Stewart said,

"I'm telling you, I have a gut feeling."

She nodded, said,

"Me, too. It means I need to throw up."

18

"When you're told, 'I kid thee not,' you are about to be seriously fucked."

Jack Taylor

Regrets, phew-oh, they are a recurrent killer. I've been tormented, tortured and roasted to rosary degree by my own history. I was heading down to Feeney's in Quay Street, still that rarity, an unchanged pub with real Irish barmen. Not a Polish guy attempting. *Jesus wept.* I admire the hell out of the Polish, but shoot me, a pint of Guinness, I want it crafted. A woman in her thirties sashaying along on those crazed Louboutins, worse, in skinny jeans.

Christ.

Then as if out of the ether, the memory, grounding me to the spot outside the Four Corners. I had a reasonably good friend, we'd once played hurling together, we shared more than a few pints and that easy camaraderie of long friendship.

Yet I'd recently heard he'd been found dead in his flat, alone and unwanted. He'd been dead eight months. His flat was bang in the centre of the city. This might happen in New York, you'd think.

Yeah, how the shit goes down in large cities.

But Galway?

I realized,

This is who I am, the guy who didn't check on his mate.

Not all the fucking poetry in the world was going to write that line.

A limo pulled up.

Swear to God, a goddamn limo. The window rolled down and Reardon, looking like a bewildered hippy, said,

"Get in."

I didn't.

He waited, then snapped,

"You deaf?"

I said,

"Actually yes, that's why I have a fucking hearing aid, you pompous bollix."

He laughed, said,

"Ah, Taylor, no wonder you amuse me. I'll give you a hundred bucks to get in."

Fuck on a bike or a limo. I said,

"I can't be bought."

"Two hundred?"

I got in.

He said,

"Can't be bought, huh?"

I sighed.

"Not easily."

He was wearing beat-up 501s, a white worn T that proclaimed, *Grateful Dead, SA, 1977*

I thought,

Yeah, as if. The fucker wasn't even born.

A large oxygen cylinder was on the seat beside him. He said,

"A guy who thinks two hundred bucks is not being bought easy, now there's a schmuck."

He nodded at the canister, said,

"Best hangover cure in the biz."

"Where's the money?"

He seemed genuinely puzzled.

"Money?"

"The two hundred."

"You want it *now?*"

Yeah, I did.

He tapped the glass partition, got the cash from the driver, handed it to me. I didn't say thanks, asked,

"What do you want?"

He intoned,

"*I am not a man, I am a people.*"

Fuck.

He explained,

"That was said by Jorge Eliécer Gaitán, a Colombian politician, back in 1948, when my old man knew him."

He gave a lopsided grin, a sight I'd believed belonged purely to caper novels, added,

"My old man claimed to have been in the crowd when Roa put a barrage into every part of Jorge's body."

Surprising me, he reached in a pouch, produced a perfect spliff, lit it, drew deep, then said,

"The crowd beat Roa to death, tore him to pieces, said my old man."

Offered me a toke. I declined, asked,

165

"Fascinating as this history ramble is, it's of the slightest fucking interest to me, why?"

He loved it, slapped my knee.

Our neighbourhood, you did that, you lost the hand. He said,

"Ah, dude, you're just so freaking wild, rude as a rattler. I'm giving you a picture of my dear old dad so you can see where I'm coming from."

It was probably then I reckoned Reardon was truly mad, so out there he could pass for sane, and he had the wealth for sanity to be moot. He flicked the roach out the window, said,

"Let them smoke weed."

Then he began to play with a heavy gold Claddagh ring on his right hand, finally took it off, said,

"My *daddy* left me this and a shitload of major stock, especially in Bogotà. When we buried him, back in Oakland, you know what I said at his grave?"

"Thanks, Dad?"

He gave me the look, see how much I was shitting him.

A lot.

Said,

"Now, Daddy-o, you can think *inside the box*."

Save for the serious-money part, most of this was horseshit. I asked again,

"What did you want to see me for?"

The limo had stopped near Blackrock, the end of the Salthill Promenade. A storm was building across from the Aran Islands, waves beginning to lash the front with their brute intensity. He said,

"I wanted to warn you off Kelly. She's my trusted employee and all that good crap, but she's nuttier than a pack of festering Church of Latter Day Saints. Apologies to Romney, etc."

For some reason I wanted to goad him, asked,

"Buying Galway, how's that going for you?"

He smiled. With the dope, it teetered on the brink of warmth. He said,

"To date, three new factories, pledges of a school, a truck full of cold cash to the Council and, hey, I'm nearly there."

I asked the obvious.

"Why?"

He opened the door, let the beginning wind swirl across our legs, said,

"Jesus, Jack, apart from the answer, *Because I can*, I thought you'd have figured out what I'm going to do."

I'd no idea, said so, and he sighed.

"Jesus H, you are a dumb fuck. I'm buying it so I can squander it."

Squander a town?

He laughed full, said,

"Don't you just fucking love it?"

19

"Rock 'n' Roll", The Velvet Underground

Has a line in there about rock 'n' roll saving her life. This may well be the ultimate Irish version of Irish irony, meaning the added sting of pure vindictiveness, posing as coincidence.

John Patrick Sheridan was thirteen years old. Ridge was thirty-nine. A bright fine Tuesday, John was rushing to school and crashed into Ridge, who was en route to collect her new car. He mumbled,

"Sorry, Ma'am."

Ma'am?

She hissed,

"Little bastard."

And they should never really have met again, but their paths had crossed and one more time they would, as it were, collide.

Neither would ever know the other, yet they would influence each other more than anything else in either of their lives. A brief footnote of interest to those of a macabre, not to say lunatic bent is that John's dad, back in the chemical day, had been a huge "underground head".

Some events are writ in water.

This chance encounter danced lightly across the Claddagh basin, reaching out towards an unremarkable bridge just outside Oranmore. But such concepts signify little but a deep longing for connection.

Meaning ultimately little but cheap coincidence and fanciful shite talk.

Stewart was sitting in my flat, looking demented. He had laid out his theory about Westbury, his certainty about the C33 victims. I'd listened as if I cared, as if I was interested. When he wound up, he asked,

"So, Jack, what do you think?"

I considered carefully, said,

"Cobblers."

Before he could argue, I said,

"Too, Westbury is a friend of mine."

Enraged, he spat,

"You have a lawyer friend?"

Now I was spitting iron, said,

"Oh, I get it. The drunk non-university bollix can't have . . ." I paused to raise sufficient venom, bitter bile, ". . . an educated friend, that it?"

He was on his feet, our friendship spiralling away, leaking all the good points like worthless euros, as close to physical confrontation as we'd ever come. He said,

"Oh, don't play the fucking working-class-hero bullshite, Jack Taylor, *man of the people*."

My mind clicked — Stewart's martial arts, his skill in kick-boxing — and figured a fast kick in the balls was the route.

He said,

"When you beat a stalker senseless a few years back . . ."

I stopped, asked,

"Yeah?"

172

The fierceness seemed to have drained away and his eyes were turned in. I wondered what was going on that I'd missed.

He continued,

"Did you feel any guilt after?"

"Sure."

He seemed relieved.

Until I added,

"Guilt I hadn't killed the fucker when I had the chance."

He shook his head, went,

"Always the hard arse."

Times I'd been called this — called worse, in truth — and did ask my own self if there was validity.

I like that.

Validity.

Such self-examination usually rode point with a few Jamesons under my conscience and the answer was mostly

"Not hard enough."

Stewart asked,

"How about this? If I find a bit more evidence on Westbury, something else connecting him to the victims, will you reconsider?"

"Yeah, yeah, whatever." My mind on the Euro Qualifiers, Ireland against Croatia. The country needed this championship so badly. Stewart followed soccer, but in that academic way that annoys the shit out of a true believer. He *analysed* games, played like you would snooker, never the shot before him but the ones to come. Sure enough, he'd said,

"It's Spain I worry about, then Italy."
I'd said,
"They'd love you in Croatia."
"Why?"
"You have us already beaten."
The ferocious vibe between us had stepped down a notch. It was there, simmering but blunted. He grabbed his jacket, said,
"Always good to chat with you, Jack."
Did I have to have the last word?
Yeah, said,
"A friend in need is God's version of *The Apprentice*."

20

"No more things should be presumed to exist than are absolutely necessary."

The law of Occam's Razor

The serial number on the bike that C33 found all those years ago?

PT290.

It would be years later when, by a series of odd coincidences, C33 was listening to the tapes of Bob Keppel with Ted Bundy, hours before they fried Bundy. Bundy had been confessing for hours, hoping to buy another reprieve. Down to the wire, he confessed to the death of a little girl. He padded out his confession saying he'd abandoned her ten-speed yellow bike in Seattle, right after he'd brutally killed her. The bike was never found.

C33 had that moment of transcendence when the letters on the bike matched.

No one could ever say C33 hadn't researched the condition / malady that drove the Galway set of *reprisals*. Gacy, Dahmer, DKK, Green River Killer, all had been researched and discarded. C33 was

something else,

something more.

Believe.

A Dexter with an Irish lilt.

In C33's wallet, behind the American driving licence, was a Gothic-scripted wedge of John Burroughs:

Nature teaches more than she preaches. There are no sermons in stones. It is easier to get a spark out of a stone than a moral.

C33 had honed the art of reprisal in the States, an equal killer land of opportunity. Get a car and a Hank Williams soundtrack and you were good to go; it was rich pickings.

But,

"There is an unknown land full of strange flowers and subtle perfumes, a land of which it is joy of all joys to dream, a land where all things are perfect and poisonous."

And so Ireland, with a race of people termed by Louis MacNeice *full of low cunning*.

Where better to ply one's trade and breathe the air that nourished and ultimately betrayed its greatest writer?

Sweet vicious irony.

Reardon had summoned me to a formal meeting, meaning, he'd stressed, I wear a tie.

Fuck that.

His new official headquarters were at the Docks, in what had been earmarked for luxury apartments until the economy spat on that. Reardon's people bought it

178

for a song and change, had converted it to state-of-the-art silicon-tech efficiency. Modelled on the gig of Microsoft, Google — lots of young nerds breaking off from their consoles to whirl frisbees, chug decaffeinated frappés, do lots of high fives.

This would be nausea all of itself, but some of these kids were Irish.

Jesus.

Rob Cox, a leading American technology writer, wrote:

"Under the hoodies and the moral language lurk rapacious business people, robber barons with the same profit motive that drives all businesses and a ruthlessness that rivals history's greatest industrial bullies."

I was in Reardon's office: pennants of the Yankees, so the guy couldn't be all rotten, a pair of crass, crossed hurleys to show he was *of the people*, a hoops basket that said,

Yo, I'm down homes.

He was dressed in cargo shorts, a T that yelled,

Ashes to Ashes,

and flip-flops.

Me, in my strangulation tie, sports jacket, Farah creased pants, like some latter-day *consigliore* to these precocious kids. Reardon was slurping on a slush, I kid thee fucking not at all, and very loudly.

Teeth clenched, I asked,

"The fuck am I wearing a tie and generally coming off like a horse's arse?"

He flipped the drink container at the basket and, to my delight, missed, said,

"'Cos, dude, like, you're, you know, old."

Crossed my mind to finally say,

Fuck it,

stride out of there, dignity walking point.

But in truth, I don't really do dignity. Not in any way anyone ever noticed. Something about Reardon rubbed a primeval urge, a desire to wipe that smug smirk in the plush carpets of his state-of-the-art office. He'd reiterated over and over his wish to use me, to employ me in some capacity, so I could swallow some humiliation. I asked,

"You want to get to the point or just waffle your hippy bullshite?"

Got him.

For one brief moment, I saw the empty man, the ego that can never be stroked, the fallow ground forever barren and power that sheens but briefly.

He rallied,

"We're developing an app that will wipe the floor of iPads,

iPhones,

iWhat the fuck ever. But there is a leak. Someone in this here office, my man, is leaking to the competition."

I laughed, said,

"I love it. You want me to catch a techie, a nerd? I wouldn't even know how to talk to them, let alone know if they were stealing the family silver."

He stood up, stretched, looked out at his crew with what could only be pride and loathing, said,

"It's Skylar or Stan, my two best people. You, my errant private eye, are going to take them for drinks, show them some of unknown Galway and, in your wily way, tell which of the . . ."

He paused with a look of affection, certainly as close to love as a megalomaniac might ever get, then said,

". . . cunts is betraying me."

Then he turned to me, his face a frozen mask, said,

"And you'll do this not only because I'll pay you to the point of orgasmic ridicule, but because, if you don't, I'll burn Stewart."

I was lost, groped for an answer.

He smiled, brittle spite leaking from the corners of his mouth, said,

"People of interest —

you,

the dyke Guard,

Stewie —

I have shadowed from day one. How I get to own cities and the likes of you can barely rent."

I was so angry I could spit, asked,

"What did Stewart do?"

He was now twisting a rubber band, doing that irritating thing as if he had gum in his hands, extending and letting it blow. I wanted to kill him with the freaking band. He said,

"Ask him. I mean, you guys, tight, right? No secrets, am I right, dawg?"

I looked out at the office, asked,

"These kids, I bring them out, show them the sights and they'll just 'fess up?"

He shrugged.

"Those two are my token Americans, naive is their genetic code, they're in a foreign country. You're like a *legend*, a Waylon Jennings, not that they'd ever the fuck have heard of him, but you get my drift. Get 'em wasted, they'll want to impress you."

I moved to go, stopped, asked,

"Saying it plays like you figure, one of those kids gives it up, what will you do?"

He seemed to be actually considering his answer, then,

"I'll fucking butcher him."

On the way out, a girl looking like an escapee from *The Brady Bunch* said to me,

"Mr Taylor, I'm Skylar, I'm so buzzed."

A guy appeared alongside, looking like he was maybe twelve. I guessed Stan. He joined the chorus, blew,

"We'll have us a blast, way cool."

I thought,

Fucking shoot me now.

21

"*The comic spirit is a necessity of life, as a purge to all human vanity.*"

Oscar Wilde

Stewart had gotten an appointment with Westbury. Dressed to legal impress: the Armani suit, muted tie, Italian shoes. It sure impressed the receptionist, who asked,

"And where have you been, ducks?"

That she was close to seventy seemed not to have dented her spirit.

The office managed to combine the old-school aura of dusty desks without the desks and a bright bay window that gave a miraculous view of Lough Corrib.

As Stewart waited, she asked,

"Like a whiskey and soda while you're waiting?"

He half thought she might be serious and was sure she'd done two of said number her own self. The magazines on the table continued the dual theme. There were:

Galway Now,

Loaded,

Top GAA Stars,

Horse and Hound.

All species covered there.

Stewart was working on his story, if indeed story he decided to go with. Maybe just flush with *Why have*

four of your clients been targeted by a lunatic vigilante?
and get turfed out on his arse.

The old dear was still staring at him, asked,

"Know how long I've been working here?"

Like he gave a shit.

He said,

"No."

"Have a guess, go on, go on."

Sounding like Pauline McLynn in *Father Ted*.

He demurred with,

"Really, I have no idea," his tone suggesting he had
zero interest.

She sniffed, said,

"You're gorgeous but, God, you're boring."

A beat.

"You lovely people, you don't have to work at
personality, just sit and be admired, you ungrateful
pricks."

Stewart had done as much research on Westbury as
he could and, from Google and Wikipedia, both UK
and Irish entries, had amassed a picture of a blend of
Brit Atticus Finch and the total headbanger of a
counsel in *Breaking Bad*.

The receptionist, whose name he saw was Ms Davis,
said,

"You can go in now. Gerald is expecting you."

Gerald!

Gerald's office was a Hollywood lawyer's space as
envisaged by Kenneth Anger. Chaos fuelled by
adrenaline. Westbury was a barrel of a man in his fifties,
all the years compressed into a tight ball of ferocious

energy. Wearing a striped shirt, loud tie, and, get this, braces, like Gecko had never gone to prison. Bald, brute head and a face that was not lived in but downright occupied. By very bad events.

He emerged from behind a desk laden with documents, hand extended.

"Mr Sandler."

"It's Stewart."

Westbury's grip was one of those duels, but Stewart from years of martial arts could hand-fuck all day. Westbury said,

"Ms Davis said you were Sandler."

Feeling like Jack, he said,

"She was wrong."

Let it hang there.

Westbury cleared a mess of files off a chair, said,

"Grab a pew, lad. Anything to drink?"

Stewart said,

"I'm not a lad and Ms Davis already offered me a whiskey and soda."

Got him.

Then he laughed, said,

"Touché, a sense of humour never goes astray. What can I do for you?"

Stewart debated for all of a minute, then said,

"I beat a man half to death, might need representation if the Guards trace the beating."

Be a perpetrator, like the dead four, and if Westbury was taking out his own clients in some perverted guise of bent justice, then bring it on. Westbury, displaying why he got the big bucks, countered instantly with,

"Alleged. Allegedly beat."

Stewart nodded, liked it, a lot.

Westbury handed over a sheet of paper, said,

"Fill out the personal stuff. Keep it vague — paper trails have a tendency to bite you in the arse."

He then quoted his fees and truly shocked Stewart.

Stewart had been reasonably successful in various enterprises, made some serious wedge along the way, but this, this was a revelation.

Westbury smiled, said,

"Hey, kid, you wouldn't be here if you couldn't afford it, and, let's face it, sounds like you can't afford *not* to be here."

Laughed at his own line, added,

"Lighten up, sonny, this is legal humour."

Stewart fixed him with his eyes, said,

"Let's get on the same page. I'm not

lad,

sonny,

kid,

any of those condescending terms. You charge like serious freaking weight, then I get some serious respect."

Westbury considered, his legal eyes betraying little save assessment, then,

"OK, you're a player. Tell me, where did you do your jail time?"

Got Stewart, hard. He managed,

"You Googled me?"

Westbury shrugged that off, said,

"Nope. Your whole vocabulary, attitude, the *don't diss me, homes* rap, screams of the Joy, and I'm not talking the Rapture. I mean Mountjoy, where, alas, some of my less successful cases rest."

Stewart wrote out a cheque, asked,

"What now?"

Westbury stretched, one of those all encompassing moves that brook neither finesse nor restraint, said,

"I get on to my guy in the Guards, see if you're a *person of interest*."

Stewart stood, shook his hand, said,

"Um, thank you, I think."

Was at the door when he heard,

"Yo, Stewie."

Stewart, a covert fan of *Family Guy*, didn't turn, simply raised his index finger, heard a hearty laugh.

22

"I don't see it as any fucking tragedy, my life. Everyone thought I'd be a failure and a liability."

Shane MacGowan, in reflective mode

The table was a riot of pints, shots, bowls of nuts and the ubiquitous iPhones and iPads. Skylar, Stan and me own self were in the Quays, two of the Saw Doctors giving an impromptu gig of reels, jigs and, of course, "Downtown", in that slanted Tuam fashion.

Skylar was ecstatic, gushed,

"Those dudes were, like, on *Letterman* and Jodie Foster bought them a burger."

If the two events were related, I was past caring. I was having me a time, having been convinced my industrial espionage gig was as low as I could go. But, hey, go figure. I was rolling, getting with the flow, enjoying me own self. The planet of geekdom was surprisingly interesting. Stan and I had bonded over

Breaking Bad, Series Four,

detour through the British, *The Thick of It*,

and back Stateside,

Veep,

doing that drink-fuelled dance of quoting each other with our favourite lines. Stan was ahead on *Veep* with,

"I've met some people, real people, and a lot of them are fucking idiots."

Selina Meyer, the fictional VP.

He thought I'd concede there, but I had Malcolm Tucker, gothic spin from *The Thick of It*, with,

"Please could you take this note, ram it up his hairy inbox, and pin it to his fucking prostate?"

I saw Skylar's face drop, offered,

"You want to talk, um, *Desperate Housewives, The Real Housewives of Beverly Hills*?"

My smile defused the insult and she said,

"What's a Black 'n' Tan?"

I presumed she meant the drink, else I'd be there a week foul-mouthing the band of thugs and scum sent to terrorize the Irish. I took the chance and ordered the drink. I was about to go for it when Stan said,

"Man, I'd kill for a Saw Doctors T-shirt."

Sometimes — rare to rarest, in truth — you get the stars in line. I spotted Ollie Jennings, their manager, one of life's real gentlemen in nature and personality. Called him, said to Stan,

"Ask their manager."

Headed for the bar.

Got the drinks, headed back to see Stan joining Ollie and the Saw Doctors. Skylar said,

"Oh, Lordy, he'll be unbearable now."

Drink or two in and she was weeping on my shoulder, confessing her love for Stan but how he seemed to have no interest. His sole focus, with music, was work. Then she said,

"He'd murder someone for the chance I have."

Jesus.

Just dropped it in my lap. And, worse, tomorrow she wouldn't even remember. I could have done the decent thing, steered the conversation in another direction. I liked her a lot. She could have been the daughter I'd never have. She had a sweetness, almost an innocence, that recalled Serena, but I couldn't go there. Drained my Jay, shook the memory of that little girl's death.

Skylar, concerned, asked,

"Mr Taylor, you OK? You seemed like you saw a ghost."

"Fucking Black 'n' Tans."

I hesitated, then,

"So, you have a shot at something big?"

She did.

Spilled it all, between drinks, a crying jag, a hint of pride and an awful shitload of indiscretion.

Some time later, Stan came back with a big, dopey grin, as happy as it Guinness gets, asked,

"How you guys doing?"

I gave him my best smile, the one that has as much ice as sparkle, said,

"We're having us one of them memorable chats."

Skylar blubbered, threw an arm round me, sobbed,

"I'll never forget this night, Mr Taylor."

I said,

"I can guarantee that, hon."

Next morning, my hangover had been curtailed by the gallon of water I'd drunk the night before. In a bizarre way, my cold manipulation of the girl had prevented me getting wasted. Jesus, I'd downed enough booze to fell the Irish rugby team, but it had been one of those evenings when the more I put away, the clearer my mind became.

A line of poetry unreeling in my head:

Your first betrayal was the coldest one.

I had a mug of black coffee, sitting in my armchair, looking out at nothing save the nasty act I'd danced along to. Reardon had been clear about what he'd do,
destroy the fucker
being one of the mildest terms he'd employed about the kid who was selling him out.

And true, the deal Skylar had been offered by Rogue Tech was a show-stopper. She'd indeed be set for life, and all she had to do was score a sizeable hit on Reardon's research. It would, she'd said,

"Put Reardon back at least eighteen months. In the tech world, that's like a death blow."

I had no doubt of my own capabilities. I'd done worse, with little aforethought.

I phoned Kelly, asked,

"How are you on moral dilemmas?"

She laughed, said,

"Shaky. You need help?"

Did I?

I said,

"Be nice to buy you a late-morning breakfast."

She said,

"We call it brunch."

"Yeah, well, here we call it a cheap lunch."

23

"Hysteria is very rarely a spectator sport."

KB

A new hotel had opened off Eyre Square just as the boom died; the hotel died soon after. Kelly asked if I'd meet her in the lobby there. I said,

"That hotel has been sold."

She laughed, said,

"Yeah, to Reardon, like most of the town, sooner than later."

I'd some time before our meet so caught up on the football. Bad to saddest worst. Irish style. Out, after three games. All the hopes, aspirations, the Trapattoni worship, ashes now.

1. Croatia beat us 3-1
2. Spain beat us 4-0
3. Italy beat us 2-0

Jesus.

And the rugby, somehow we'd pull consolation out of the European fiasco with them, but against the Kiwis we had an all-time record-breaking defeat.

Sixty-*nil*.

Dazed, I'd watched England against Italy go to penalty shootout and, argh, the Brits lost. My sympathies had been with Hart, the English goalie. To have to watch the ferocious Balotelli bear down on goal was to see Armageddon in a blue shirt.

But, hey, you take comfort where any crumb is available. Right?

The European bridge championships were being held to considerably less fanfare and we were in the quarter-finals.

That mattered, didn't it?

Preparations for the Volvo Ocean Race were in full pace, the race terminating in Galway in a few short weeks. As I waited in the hotel lobby for Kelly, I read through the city preparations to receive the yachts. Meant a sizeable payday to the city. No wonder Clancy and the city hotshots refused to entertain the concept of C33, a vigilante running loose with world media lurking. No, had to keep that bogey under wraps.

Heard,

"Yo, sailor."

Kelly, dressed in tight white jeans, tight black T-shirt, her face radiant. I felt the stir if not of echoes then yearning. She leaned over to do that ridiculous air kiss, then suddenly veered to a real kiss, her tongue deep in my mouth, then withdrew, said,

"Suck that."

Jesus.

A waitress appeared, looking all of sixteen and suddenly making Kelly seem . . . extreme? Kelly snapped,

"Lolita, get us a pot of coffee before the yachts arrive."

I said, recovering some tarnished dignity,
"You have the essentials of leadership down."
She gave me a mischievous grin, asked,
"What would they be, *mon amour?*"
"Rudeness and hostility."
She laughed as the coffee came, said to the girl,
"Put it on Reardon's tab."
The girl was confused, waited.
I said,
"He owns the hotel."
She lit up, went,
"Oh, *Mr* Reardon."
Kelly sat back, said,
"Take a hike."
I asked,
"Are you working on being a bitch, or is it, you know, natural?"
Gave me a long look, asked,
"Long as the bitch is in your corner, what do you care?"
I told her about my dilemma, Skylar being headhunted and her selling out Reardon. She gave me an odd look, asked,
"What's the dilemma?"
Truth to tell, I wanted to look like I was at least having a struggle with this; like somewhere in me was a streak of decency. I said,
"Well, she's a nice kid. Seems like she *confided* in me, and to just sell her seems *cold*."
She laughed out loud, said,

"How the fuck do you know what's she like? She didn't confide in you, she got wasted, shot her mouth off."

Jesus, was I sorry I'd asked. I said,

"Betrayal is not only a shitty thing to do, it's . . . it's un-Irish."

She loved that, tapped my head, said,

"'Fess up, buddy, you want to look noble while being a cunt."

The sun had come out, maybe in anticipation of the Volvo Ocean Race. Kelly said,

"Walk with me."

We headed down towards the Corn Market. Kelly said,

"I love this city. It's so walker friendly."

I sniffed,

"Tell it to *Lonely Planet*."

She stopped, said,

"You have the weirdest thought processes. I mean, you seem rational, then wham-o, you're off on some side trip, like a Seth MacFarlane with Irish sensibility."

Fuck, *Family Guy* I wasn't. I said,

"*Lonely Planet* stuck it to the city, big time."

She gave that enigmatic smile, signifying little, said,

"Those dudes handed you your ass, right?"

In a word, yes.

We were outside Charlie Byrne's, a display of noir crime novels in the window, including:

El Niño,

Absolute Zero,

The Point,
The Twelve,
The Cold, Cold Ground.
Vinny was just heading in, laden with books. He
shouted,
"Yo, Jack, a hand, eh?"
Kelly glanced at my mutilated fingers and nodded,
and I went to help Vinny. He looked at Kelly and raised
his left eyebrow. I said,
"She's American."
He manoeuvred the door, got the box in, said,
"'Course she is, Jack. She's with you."
Go figure!
Kelly bought *The Collected Works of Oscar Wilde.*
It was in beautiful condition, leather binding, gilt pages.
The price?
Vinny said,
"Five euros."
Kelly went,
"You're kidding. It's worth ten times that."
He gave that Vinny smile, the one that says,
You love books, we love you.
I found a copy of John Lahr's *New Yorker* profiles.
We'd just got outside, her mobile shrilled, sounding
like "Home of the Brave".
I could hear a raised voice. She grimaced, then
passed the phone to me, said,
"Your master's voice."
Reardon, snarling.
"I expected a report this morning."
I said,

"Here's a report. Fuck you."

Clicked off. Then asked her,

"Oh, sorry, were you finished?"

She sighed.

"You certainly are."

Then she offered the Wilde book, said,

"For you."

"No, thanks. Such learning would only foul the genetic pool."

She asked,

"You know what happens to people who refuse gifts?"

"No."

Her departing smile.

"Ah, the not knowing . . . that's the beauty of it. Dinner this evening, my treat."

I watched her walk away, that assured strut, a woman who owned her space, and if you wanted to invade, you better bring your very best game.

Later, I watched the semi-final, Italy *vs.* Germany, Balotelli like a gift from the God of Football, until my doorbell went.

Reardon.

A riled Reardon, with a hulking guy behind him. He said,

"That's Leo, my protection."

I said,

"Leo gets to protect the space *outside* my flat."

Leo growled and Reardon didn't like it much better, but agreed, came in, glanced at the screen, said,

"Fucking wops need niggers to win a game."

I said,

"Yo, shithead, you want to do redneck crap, do it outside, with your gorilla."

He laughed, said,

"Leo doesn't like you."

I went to the fridge, cracked open a couple cold ones, handed him one, said,

"Leo's likes are way down on my current concern list."

Reardon was dressed in the Galway hurling jersey, combat shorts and I think they call his footwear espadrilles. They looked comfortable and, best, worn. He flopped down on my second-best chair, said,

"So, Taylor, spill."

Meaning, the goods on Skylar.

I clinked his bottle, said,

"*Sláinte.*"

Never meant it less. If you could lightly wish *Roast in hell* it would have been closer.

I asked,

"So what have you got on Stewart?"

Reardon was scanning the apartment, missing nothing, said,

"Enough to send his supercilious ass to the slammer."

I sipped the beer, continued,

"So, the deal is, I drop the dime on your employee, you let Stewart slide?"

Reardon looked at me, said,

"Jesus H. How many times you want me to say it? Yes."

I was working my way up to divulging Skylar's name when he muttered,

"Fucking Skylar. I thought that kid would have been more savvy. If it was Stan, I'd get it. He's just a dopey geek."

What?

I said,

"Skylar! You know! How the fuck do you know?"

He flipped the empty bottle high. It hovered dangerously for a moment, then landed in the waste basket with a heavy thud. He said,

"Gotcha."

Smiled, then,

"Oh, Kelly told me."

Jesus, these fucking people. I near shouted,

"Why would she tell you?"

He laughed, got to his feet in one fluid click, said,

"We used to be married."

She'd told me she'd never been married.

Relishing my stunned dumb expression, he said,

"Lesson one, pal, wherever you think you've been, us rich guys, we've already had that and — guess what? — discarded it."

Len Waters was from a very good home; best background, in fact. Family lived in Taylor's Hill, father a surgeon, mother a hypocrite, best schools, almost university, trust fund, reasonably good looking, twenty years of age and a psychopath.

206

He was a run-of-the-mill nut job, possessing none of the attributed charm these fucks could exercise. His kick was to barge in on old women, beat them to a pulp, and any other vile act his cesspool mind could conjure. Maybe due to chance, he hadn't yet murdered anyone, least anyone that somebody missed.

Now in custody, he was facing three charges. Westbury was his lawyer and in jig time had the skel out on bail. Stewart had followed all this diligently, convinced that Waters was the perfect victim for C33. If Westbury and C33 were one and the same, Stewart would be there to witness it. After Waters had been released amid a flurry of indignation, near riots and press reportage, Stewart arranged an appointment with Westbury, claiming it was urgent and managing to meet him in a pub. This is not so difficult if you agree that pub hours, too, are on their clock.

They get drinks, get paid, who's hurting?

Westbury arrived in McSwiggan's dressed in victory and Armani, his face flush from trumping the legal system again. Stewart had grabbed a table at the back, offered,

"Champagne?"

Westbury was tempted, then,

"No, maybe a little early for celebration, so a large gin and tonic."

No ice. A serious drinker.

Stewart had a large glass of lime and water, could pass for the real thing. He touched Westbury's glass, said,

"Congrats. You're good."

Westbury, who'd obviously had a few at the office, his face flushed, slight beads of perspiration on his brow, scoffed,

"Good? I'm the freaking best, sonny."

OK.

Ego checked.

Stewart said,

"I wanted to check on my own status, but also buy you a drink to show my appreciation of you taking an interest when you are . . ."

Paused.

"So brilliantly busy."

Almost overdid it.

Westbury paused too, reassessed Stewart, then, mollified, said,

"There is a simple secret to even the darkest allegation."

Stewart was fascinated by Westbury's bullet-proof confidence, wondered if it had to do with the fact that, if he was indeed the C33 vigilante, the outcome of any case was irrelevant as he administered the final justice and got paid, too. Win / win.

He echoed,

"Secret?"

Westbury was waving to various high-profile types who passed, basking in his current success, said,

"Money."

Stewart couldn't be bothered arguing the toss. He thought this might be true to a degree, but wouldn't want to be in the dock hoping cash was the key.

Westbury said,

"I made some discreet inquiries of the Guards and currently you are not a person of interest."

Stewart acknowledged his debt, said,

"I'd still like to retain you lest something arise in the future."

Westbury's mobile shrilled, he answered, made some *Mmm* noises, then stood, said,

"Duty calls."

They shook hands. Westbury said,

"Stay in touch."

And turned as he was leaving, added,

"Stay in funds."

24

"The black affliction of the brain."

Bertolt Brecht

Kelly climbed out of my bed, looked back, said,

"What you lack in heat you make up for in desperation."

Add that to a fragmented ego, see how it plays. I sat up on one elbow, like Matthew McConaughey seems to do in every movie, but I did skip the squeezing of my eyes. She was doing that thing women think is cute:

wearing the guy's shirt.

Drives guys mental.

It was also my prized multi-washed cotton work shirt.

I said,

"So, you were married to Reardon."

She pulled her bag over, took out a pack of Virginia Slims, lit one with a solid gold Zippo, that clunk sounding, as it always did, like some weary hope. She blew out a cloud of smoke, said,

"You've been holding that for a time, measuring the max impact."

She was caught between annoyance and amusement, continued,

"He comes from . . ."

She paused,

asked,

"You know the term, *fuck-you money?*"

Sure.

"Well, his family is so far up that fuck-you trail they don't even bother to brag about it, they just do it: annihilate and move on. I come from jack shit, and to get in that charmed circle I'd have fucked his whole clan."

This riled me in ways I couldn't even articulate. I spat,

"So did you? Lay the whole crew?"

She dropped the cig in my coffee cup — and, no, I wasn't finished — said,

"Pretty much."

She was heading for the shower. I asked,

"You must have done pretty fine from the divorce."

She looked at me in genuine puzzlement.

"Who got divorced?"

She switched on the TV, the final of the Volvo Ocean Race at the Galway Docks. Eighty thousand people turned up at two in the morning to welcome them. New Zealand was first over the line but the French won on overall time. It was to be the beginning of nine days of party-on in Galway and a huge financial coup to the city.

She flicked it off, said,

"Reardon's got a boat."

Jesus, *quelle surprise.* Like I gave a good fuck.

I asked,

"In the race?"

She laughed, began to make coffee, said,

"Yeah, right, like the dude's got the time to sail round the world. It's berthed in Saint-Tropez, or is it Saint-Malo?"

I asked, edge leaking over my tone,

"Remind me again why you're with me?"

She glanced up, asked,

"You don't know?"

Dare to hope.

Said,

"I make you laugh?"

She sighed as she surveyed my range of coffee, said,

"Slumming, see how a loser lives."

There was no smile on her lips.

And certainly no warmth in her tone.

I'd recently come across the first of Arne Dahl's novels to be translated into English, *The Blinded Man*. A passage in there captured a look that passed between Kelly and me as she handed me a mug of coffee.

Did those few minutes in the kitchen draw them closer together? Or had a final chasm opened up between them? It was impossible to say, but something decisive had taken place; they had looked into each other's naked loneliness.

So many times, a passage from a book reflected exactly the current of my life.

But never did my life reflect a single piece of uplifting writing in all my reading years. My life didn't imitate fiction; it mocked it.

★ ★ ★

A memorial was unveiled in Celia Griffin Park to honour the victims of the Famine ships, and those rescue ships that had tried so hard to deliver our people to the US. Celia Griffin was six years old during the Famine and died of hunger on the streets of Galway. An autopsy revealed she had not a scrap of food in her stomach.

Mark Kennedy had

cajoled,

struggled,

fought,

to raise the funding for this memorial, and, close to his seventy-sixth birthday, he saw his dream fulfilled. How fitting it was attended by Brian Sheridan, the Harbour Master, as he juggled with the logistics of the Volvo Ocean Race.

Truly, a shard of sunshine amid so much darkness.

Don Stiffe had composed a song for the occasion, titled

"Song for Celia".

And there, in the sunshine, he sang it as the audience, their eyes wet, turned out towards Galway Bay. Kelly had come along with me. I had promised to show her a slice of real Galway and she went,

"Dead kid, huh?"

I wanted to wallop her.

Len Waters' apartment was beyond basic. Someone with money and spare time had attacked it with clichés. The mega flat screen, heavy leather sofa, kitchen outfitted with every expensive gadget, never used. Lads' mags scattered on the glass coffee table and obligatory ashtray with butts and spliff ends. The fridge had simply six packs and a half bottle of Grey Goose.

C33 was partial to a chilled vodka, found new Waterford crystal in a cupboard and poured a decent measure. Sat on the couch, feet up on the table and wondered what anxiety was like. Having recently read about it in a medical column, it seemed like a useful vibe to imitate.

Too, it could double up with stress and have a whole concerned presentation running. C33 placed the shotgun on the sofa, double O ammunition. Bought in that fish and tackle shop without any fuss. Even exchanged pleasantries.

"Shame about the weather."

"Indeed."

And on leaving heard,

"God bless the hunting."

Gotta love that.

C33 thought about Waters, wondered if there was any point in a chat before offing the little bastard. The guy terrorized old women, working his twisted path towards the main event. What was there to talk about?

The vodka was slipping down easy, a nice glow building. C33 thought about Jack Taylor and knew now that he was not going to be an ally. Had seemed like an idea to play with him, him being such a book fiend. But he had failed to follow up on the clues, and now seemed more interested in his limp romance.

C33 sighed.

Stewart. Now maybe that's the way the game should have gone. Stewart was definitely willing to rap, but C33 shouted,

"So goddamn freaking slow."

Needed everything spelled out?

Fucksakes!

A key turned in the door. C33 breathed,

"Showtime."

Len Waters had been on the piss, big time. A fairly average evening for him.

Barred from three pubs,

thrown out of two clubs,

one fistfight outside Supermac's,

and threw up twice near the canal.

Whatever company he'd been in had abandoned him. Nothing new there. He was just trouble without the humour. Now Waters was hit by the late-night appetite for something

greasy,

full of fat,

cheap,

and had no money.

Fuck.

Thought back in his kip of a flat he had some stashed coke. Yeah, get some lines done, then he'd see. Maybe head back out, smash some old bitch up, yeah, get right in her old face, crush it. That never got old.

Took him a few minutes to get his key aligned with the lock and involved a stream of obscenities, then literally fell in. He lay on the floor, unable to get up for a moment, and started to laugh for no reason other than simple derangement.

A voice cut through his mirth.

"Care to share the joke?"

C33 had decided to go with one barrel, as one was more than sufficient to wipe Waters off the map. All the talk C33 had planned on giving had just evaporated and he thought,

Who the fuck can be bothered?

And what could Waters have possibly said of vague interest?

Standing over the body, he nudged the head with a boot. Dead as a doornail. The smell of cordite was intoxicating. C33 looked round the flat, shrugged and opened the door, the shotgun cradled on the right arm.

A man standing outside stared at C33, struggling to place the face, said,

"I know you."

The movement,

shotgun,

one,

moved fast to the right hand,

two,

finger on the trigger,

three,

second barrel goes

into Stewart's face.

25

"*Artists certainly aren't easy people.*"

"No," *Eva giggled,* "*but somebody's got to take the trouble to emphasize the depths of existence so that the rest of you have a surface to skate over.*"

Karin Fossum, *In the Darkness*

"*Purgatory is the back-up plan the Church has for Hell.*"

KB

I was watching Season Five of *Breaking Bad* when I heard the knock at the door. Expecting Kelly, I ran my fingers through my hair. Make an effort, right? Smile in place, I opened the door to Ridge.

A very distressed Ridge. Could see her red eyes, knew it must be bad. If Ridge was crying it was hard core. I ushered her in, got her sitting down, waited.

She said,

"Stewart's been shot."

That didn't make any sense. Not Stewart, the guy was too fast, too aware. I muttered,

"What?"

"He was found at the home of a young guy who'd been killed. We think he may have disturbed the killer."

I couldn't get a handle, tried,

"What young guy? Jesus, where . . . I mean, how is he, Stewart?"

She stared down at the floor. I grabbed her shoulder, rougher than I intended, shouted,

"Ridge?"

"He's dead, Jack."

★ ★ ★

The next few days were a flurry of dazed and utter confusion. I was there, present, but only barely. For some fucked-up reason, Stewart had named me as his next of kin in his papers. He had to be kidding, but kidding wasn't anything he'd be doing again. I knew he'd lost all contact with his family after his jail time, but to name me, Jesus, what was he thinking?

Like everything else, he'd arranged his *disposal*, as he termed it in his will.

Cremation.

"He was afraid of small spaces," Ridge told me.

How'd she get told and not me?

You want cremation in Galway, it makes perfect Irish sense, you have to travel to Dublin. Fuck. In my anger, I'd spat,

"Hey, give me a can of petrol and a Zippo, we can stay home."

Ridge let that slide.

Kelly had said,

"Anything you need?"

Yeah, my friend back.

She got Reardon to arrange a flight to Dublin, and Ridge, Stewart and I made the trip early on the Monday morning before the Races. We were back that evening, with Stewart in an urn. All of that is only vaguely recallable, brief vignettes of pain and anger. I was drinking but not drunk, not sober and certainly not in any sane state of mind.

Phew-oh.

I do remember the plane ride back, Stewart on the seat beside me. I asked Ridge, who was as shell-shocked as my own self,

"What do we do with the urn? Put it on our mantelpieces, take it alternate weekends?"

She shook her head, said,

"He left instructions."

Of course.

Ridge and I were waiting close to Nimmo's Pier, a boat due to take us out on the bay to scatter Stewart. I'd handed the urn to Ridge, felt weird holding my friend thus. Ridge looked down at it, said,

"And I've held you in the palm of my hand."

It was shortly before noon, the Claddagh church would soon be ringing the bell for the Angelus. I was burning with bitterness, bile and bewilderment.

I said,

"Who'd ever think I'd outlive Stewart?"

Ridge gave me an unknowable look, said,

"You shouldn't have, no way."

Jesus, steady.

A lone swan came gliding along. Ridge watched it with longing, said,

"They say a swan is the reincarnation of a Claddagh fisherman who drowned."

Fuck.

I said.

"Jesus, I'm so tired of Irish

piseógs,

stories,

omens,

superstitions,

fairy fucking tales.

Stewart is fucking dead and he ain't coming back as a swan or any other freaking thing."

Like I said,

bitterness oozing.

I'd checked out Len Waters. He fitted the bill for the C33 agenda but the Guards were no way going the way of a vigilante and, anyway, Stewart had been a dope-dealer. Never fucking mind it was years ago, he was dirty, end of story. Waters *and Stewart* had been clients of Westbury, and Stewart had told me he was trying to find a link between Westbury and the former victims. And I'd

. . . blown him off.

I said to Ridge,

"Stewart thought the lawyer, Westbury, was worth investigating, maybe even building a case for him being the C33 character."

Ridge shook her head.

"It's nothing. The Guards checked out all this nonsense, there is no link between the killings."

Fuck sake.

I said,

"What about the notes?"

She gave me the look, then,

"There's a school of thought that, um, that suggests you might have written those."

"Are you fucking kidding? Why? Why on earth would I do that?"

The boat was approaching. I moved back from the pier, asked,

"And you, Ridge, what *school* do you favour?"

She said,

"You've been under lots of pressure and maybe, you know, a desire to look, um . . . significant, in front of your American buddies."

She put a lean of condescension on *buddies*.

I started to move away.

She asked,

"Where are you going? We have to scatter Stewart's ashes."

I fixed my eyes on her, tried to keep my voice low, said,

"You're smart, just take the top off and *scatter*."

My mind was in freefall.

A line from Scott Walker — he'd said something like this was how you vanished.

To a torrent of self-recrimination, a chorus of not disapproval but downright bile, thinking,

I always knew when the joke was over, but my dilemma?

Never being quite sure when it began.

Towards David Mamet describing his childhood,

In the days prior to television, we liked to while away the evenings by making ourselves miserable, solely based on our ability to speak the language viciously.

Pause.

Stopped to catch my breath, reach for my cigarettes, and,

"Fuck, don't smoke no more."

Fume, yes, freely and with intent. The director Mike Nichols declaring,

I do well with the fundamentally inconsolable.

Fucking A.

A homeless person asked me for something and I shouted,

"You want something? Here, a word of consolation, fuck off."

Repented.

Went back.

Gave him a fifty euro, heard him mutter,

"Bloody eejit."

26

"It's over for you, motherfucker."

The voice Brian Wilson heard in his head,
over and over, for twenty years.

I went down into the abyss,
    spiral
    screaming
                    burning hot
    to
    freakish
            cold
    fucked.
Snatches of Stewart's friendship flashing through my mind like dire recriminations of what would never be again. Five days before I surfaced, kind of, through sickness like I'd rare to rarer experienced.

I came to in my own apartment, a large man sitting opposite, lounging in a chair, drinking from one of my coffee mugs, a slight smile playing on his lips. I didn't know if he was real, or part of the previous day's horrors and hallucinations. I croaked,

"Hey."

Deep, yeah.

I sat up, real bad idea. The room did a jig, a reel. The man stood, got a glass of water, said,

"Get some of this down, slow 'n' easy."

I did, slowly, and managed to keep some of it down. I asked,

"Who are you?"

He was even bigger when my vision settled, over six-two and climbing. And must have been close to two hundred pounds, not much of it fat. A face that had been squatted in then grilled. Cold blue eyes, but with a shot of amusement. Wearing chinos and black, battered Doc Martens, the originals. A T-shirt with the logo

MONTEREY ROCKS

so faded it might have been an original, which could mean he'd seen Jimi Hendrix. I shook my head as he said,

"Name is Moore, least that's we're giving out today."

And he smiled, kind of.

He said,

"I've got some healing here for you, buddy, some pills your benefactor Mr Reardon provided."

Reardon?

Moore had been asked by Reardon to keep an eye on me, mainly for Kelly's sake, and found me crumpled in a mess outside my apartment, reeking to high heaven of booze. Got me inside and halfway cleaned up.

I snapped,

"So, have I to beg? Let's make with the fucking things or not."

He laughed, took out a battered tin, began to roll a cig. I said,

"No-smoking zone, pal."

He laughed again, said,

"I like it, and gotta say, dude who's taken the punishment you have, to crack funny, that's hardcore."

He, I kid thee not, flicked a long match off his boot, lit up. I said,

"You're kidding. What, you studied Clint movies and then figured you'd trot out that party trick?"

He blew a perfect ring, said,

"Just a match, partner, nothing more."

Jesus, I'd woken up in a scene from a clichéd Western by freaking numbers. He reached in his pocket, tossed a phial and, no, I didn't catch it. Fuck.

Got the lid off, got two capsules out, dry swallowed them. He said,

"Trusting type, ain't yah?"

I said,

"If you're poisoning me, the hangover I have coming down the pike, you'd be doing me a favour."

He shrugged, said,

"You've got some grit, fellah."

I asked,

"So, who the fuck are you? And what are you doing in my home, besides cowboy cameos?"

He stood up, did the neck exercise beloved of jocks, said,

"I'm your guardian angel."

His accent was gruff, no-prisoners New York, Lower East Side if I knew my Jimmy Breslin. His eyes testified to war years with not so many bullets avoided.

I gave him my best sceptical look, honed on years of dealing with priests who told me the Kingdom of Heaven was within.

Within whom they neglected to mention.

Christ, I began to feel good, not just, um . . . hungover, but fucking real fine. I had a shower, shouted,

"Brew up some coffee there."

Pause.

"Pilgrim."

Angel dust indeed. I dressed fast, raring to go. Faded Levi's, cleanish white cotton shirt, my fave boots, the ones that clicked, made you sound like you were going places or, least, had been some joint of significance. A light jacket, khaki in colour, that gave the vibe of a player.

Being able to stand straight, I was near as tall as Moore. He handed me a steaming mug of caff, said,

"Roasted Colombian."

Roast heaven.

All I needed was spurs, a gray Palomino and *wagons fucking ho* to be the full cowboy.

Moore was surveying me, then pulled out a small jotter and with a stub of a pencil made some notes. No Mont Blanc posing here. I asked,

"You taking notes?"

Growled,

"Sure as shooting."

Show time. Asked,

"Why?"

"For Mr Reardon. He sicced me on you, to keep your dumb ass safe."

He saw my expression, said,

"Smell the beans, *compadre*. You're a guinea pig. Those pills, you're . . ."

He chuckled.

"straight out . . ."

Fucking chuckled.

". . . the trial subject."

Added,

"Used to be there was gold in them thar hills."

Breath.

"Now, it's pharmaceuticals, the big dipper, the treasure of the Sierra Madre, all rolled in one. Can you imagine having a real live test subject, not in a goddamn lab but out on the street, living it, if not large, at least colourful? The FDA will be shitting themselves."

I was horrified, but buoyed by the dope.

Managed,

"He's using me as a guinea pig?"

He made a gun of his hand, let the thumb / hammer fall. I managed,

"Jesus, wait till Kelly hears this."

He laughed, said,

"Her idea."

It was out before I could think.

"The cunt."

Wagged a finger in my face, said,

"Easy, partner, that's my sister you're dissing."

God on a bloody unbelievable bike. I muttered,

"Jesus, you people all related?"

He smiled, said,

"Like to roll our own."

And,

"Tell you what, *caballero*. Those pills should be kicking in and I hear give you an appetite, so how's about I treat you to some eggs over easy, bacon, pot of Joe?"

Truth to tell, I was now ravenous, said,

"Sure, long as I can have me some grits."

He looked at me, asked,

"They do grits?"

"Get fucking real, Clint."

The pills coasted me back to the land of hunger, near normality and light. Moore sighed, said,

"I can see you're improved, and it's time we grabbed some chow."

He was out the door, his boots echoing in the hall like a rumour that was only half understood. I caught up with him on the street, said,

"Tell you what, I'll buy breakfast, see if you can open up a bit about Reardon."

He gave a non-committal grunt.

The GBC do the best fry-up.

Lots of neon cholesterol,

runny eggs,

fat Clonakilty sausages,

black pudding like the Pope ordered (cross me heart),

thick streaky rashers,

and a pot of Barry's tea like the childhood you never had.

I ordered all of this for two and then, under the table, pushed the snub-nosed .38 to him, said,

"Think you mislaid this."

He reached for his back, from where I'd relieved him of it during my *stumble*. He was as close to impressed as a stone jackal got, asked,

"You learn that in the Guards?"

I waved at Frank Casserly, the chef, then said,

"I learned it on the streets."

The tea and thick buttered toast arrived and he asked,

"So, want to know what you missed while you were . . . away . . . for five days?"

I had to focus, trying to measure how long it had been since Stewart . . . since Stewart. Said,

"The Olympics."

He poured the strong tea, bit down on a hefty wedge of dripping toast, said,

"You guys got five medals, gold for the Taylor lass in boxing."

Jesus.

"Really?"

"Yup, no shit, Sherlock, you guys can fight."

The food arrived, freaking mountains of it. Moore said,

"Man, gonna flood some major arteries here."

But he dug in, like he had a shovel rather than a fork. He said,

"Lots of folks bought the farm while you were AWOL."

I felt the food lodge in my throat, spat,

"Besides my best friend?"

He shrugged, said,

"Yeah, well, condolences and all that good shit. Gore Vidal, Helen Gurley Brown, Ernest Borgnine."

Like I could give a fuck.

I said,

"So you're to babysit while I'm running on experimental meds."

He was having a second mug of tea, seemed to be liking it, said,

"Reardon wants to ensure you don't end up like your best bud."

"I'm touched."

He laughed, said,

"Hell, Taylor, you ain't shit to shinola to him, but Kelly, she seems to have some weird shine on you. Go figure, huh?"

I simply muttered,

"C33."

He stopped.

Actually held his mug mid-frozen, asked,

"What did you say?"

I was about to tell him about Westbury and he grabbed my arm, snarled,

"Not the whole fucking saga, the number, you said a number."

"C33."

He put the mug down, shaken, murmured,

"I'll be fucking hog-tied."

"What?

"That's the name of the pills — the crap you're swallowing."

★ ★ ★

I think that's what they call a *showstopper*.

Jesus.

My mind racing to all sorts of scenarios.

Reardon was C33?

Playing at vigilantism like he fucked around with everything else. And what a perfect rat fuck, to dabble in serial killing. Just the kind of sick shit he'd relish. Would explain the initial letters to me. Reardon was stuck in every aspect of my life. Did Stewart surprise him and just happen to be collateral damage?

As my mind jumped through a myriad mazes, Moore stood up, said,

"Gotta go jam my head under some real cold water."

The bill was on the table. I said,

"You picking up the tab?"

He grimaced, said,

"Been picking up the freight on you for five days, hoss. Time you paid some dues."

He was heading out. I said,

"Moore?"

"Yeah?"

"Don't call me *hoss* again."

27

"Like most people raised on American movies, I have poor access to my emotions but can banter like a motherfucker."

Josh Bazell, *Wild Thing*

"Rumour is always more exciting than truth."

KB

I was in Crowe's pub on Prospect Hill, the borderline between that and Bohermore probably the only true neighbourhoods remaining in the city. Like the awful theme from *Cheers*, people here *did know your name*.

Ollie Crowe was arranging a post party for the crowds attending Eamonn Deacy's testimonial and a young guy near me was regaling his girl with a line from the new Joan Rivers biography.

Like this:

Joan Rivers' mother asked the doctor, "Will the baby live?"

Meaning Joan.

"Not unless you take your foot off her throat."

His girl looked at him, asked,

"Joan who?"

A guy was staring at a pint of Guinness as if he might find some answer, then looked at me, said,

"You hear about the new trend?"

Jesus, kidding or what?

Could be anything from the Rose of Tralee being fixed to Galway losing the minor semi-final.

It wasn't.

He said,

"Mirror fasting."

I asked,

"What the fuck are you on about?"

He smirked, delighted to have that Irish prized possession, knowledge, especially knowledge *you* don't have, said,

"Women are trying not to look in mirrors for certain amounts of time, as it only pressures them if they do it daily."

I'd have laughed if my spirit wasn't so overladen.

Ridge arrived looking forlorn, but gorgeous. Dressed in a black leather jacket, black jeans, boots, she could have passed for a mild dominatrix. I kept that to myself, asked,

"Get you something?"

Her eyes were on fire. I knew I'd be catching some sparks. She said,

"Your answer to everything, a drink."

Spurred,

"Not really. I was just trying to inject some civility."

She gave a bitter smile, said,

"Make a nice change."

The guy who'd made the Joan Rivers joke leaned over, asked,

"That your wife?"

Shocking the bejaysus out of us equally.

I said,

"God forbid."

Added,

"Maybe a bit of mirror fasting, eh?"

Her face was a blend of bile and reined violence.

I did the real smart thing: I began to leave. Ridge, in that bitch mode, headed for the street, fast. She snapped,

"Where are *you* going?"

I turned, stared, said,

"The hell away from you, Sergeant."

"Superintendent Clancy wants to talk to you, and I mean *now*."

"Tell him I was doing my usual solving."

"What?"

"You know, drinking."

She grabbed my arm. I looked at her hand, said,

"Bad idea."

She let go, asked,

"Please?"

Ground it out between her teeth.

I smiled, said,

"See, not so hard. Let's go see the Super."

Clancy and I had such bad history, we nigh forgot most of the reasons he hated me. Dressed in his full true blues, he cut an impressive figure, least he thought so. I said,

"Been watching Tom Selleck, I guess."

He surveyed me, not much liking a single thing he saw, said,

"This C33 nonsense you're spreading has got to stop."

I sighed, then,

"Best tell that to C33 is my shot."

He shuffled some papers, said,

"You might remember I told you we were investigating some cold cases."

Let me savour that. He'd threatened to show that my beloved dad had stolen from the railway pension fund, destroy any decency our fragmented family weakly held. Now he let me see which way I wanted to jump.

As if I'd a whole load of choice. I asked,

"And for the . . . um . . . railway case not to be a priority, so to speak?"

He smiled, a thing of pure ugliness, said,

"I'm surmising your interest in C33 is waning."

I asked,

"Who's C33?"

He leaned back in his leather chair, said,

"Run along, there's a good lad."

The Irish shit sandwich — pat your head as they kick your arse.

28

"And I am so clever that sometimes I don't understand a single word I'm saying."

Oscar Wilde, *The Remarkable Rocket*

I met Westbury in his office. If any of the deaths had affected him in any way, he wasn't showing it. Dressed in a suit that must have cost three fortunes, he asked,

"How exactly can I help you, Mr Taylor?"

A lawyer calls you Mister, lose your wallet as he already owns it. I said,

"Call me Jack."

Got an enigmatic smile that gave away precisely zero. He didn't extend the courtesy, so I figured we were still definitely not on first-name territory. I said,

"Just a strange coincidence. Five of the people you represented are dead. Worse, murdered."

He looked at me, then,

"Is there a question in there . . . *Jack?*"

Leaning oh so slightly on my name. No fucking with this guy. I said,

"I wondered if you'd an opinion on that?"

His smile spread, a joke he'd written the punchline for many times. He said,

"Jack, my opinion is very, very measured. You can read that as expensive."

Before I could answer, he asked,

"You are here in any, how shall I put it, legal capacity?"

Like he didn't know. I said,

"Stewart was my best friend. I don't know what *legal* weight that carries."

He shot back,

"Well, I can answer that easily and, better, not charge you. Its weight is zilch, nada, and, as they say in our native tongue, *níl rud ar bith agat*."

That last bit nicely translates as *You've fuck-all, Jack*.

Kelly was sipping a Bloody Mary in the bar at Jury's, bottom of Quay Street. I hadn't arranged to meet her. It was one of those bars where you could see the interior from the street. I'd been fuming along, simmering from Westbury, when I glanced to my right, saw her. Turned and went in. If she was glad to see me, she was hiding it well. Lunch hour was looming and I asked,

"Getting an early start?"

She was wearing a dazzling white tracksuit, her hair tied up in that no-nonsense bun that women do effortlessly. A hardcover of *The Importance of Being Oscar* was open before her. She stared at me, mused,

"Taylor or Wilde?"

Then, deciding, shut the book.

A waitress approached and I ordered a Galway sparkling water. Kelly said,

"Another of those,"

indicating her own now-finished drink. The girl asked,

"Tomato juice?"

Kelly sighed, said,

"Yeah, with a shipload of Grey Goose."

Kelly asked,

"And how are you, Jacques?"

Like a damn fool I began to tell her. During the telling, her drink arrived and finally she did that *wind it up, fellah* motion.

Said,

"Jesus, Taylor, when I asked you, I didn't really care, and guess what? I care even fucking less now."

I moved back, said,

"Phew, you really are not in a good place."

She looked at her empty glass, like,

How'd that happen?

Said,

"I'm sorry, Jack, it's just Stewart."

And trailed off.

I echoed,

"Stewart?"

She seemed to be tearing up, said,

"We'd become close. Well, Zen proximity."

Christ, she sounded like him. I asked,

"You and Stewart?"

She said,

"Not sure you were the friend to him you could have been."

And with that blow, stood, touched my face with her hand, said,

"I need to grieve."

And was gone.

Leaving me the bill and the Wilde book.

Trust me, Bloody Marys and, yeah, a sparkling water, are not cheap.

I left the book as a cheap tip and got out of there before I had to face the waitress. I was out of cash and definitely out of options.

I went after her, determined to ask about her husband, Reardon, the new drug named C33. But on Quay Street there was no sign.

Back at my flat, I cracked a beer, sat down to watch the last four episodes of *Life* (Series Two) with Damian Lewis. And you guessed it, another cancelled show. A crime. The final episode had writing and drama the equal of anything on HBO.

All of this to distract my mind, the reeling, conflicting notions:

Stewart and Kelly,

Reardon and C33,

Ridge and extreme annoyance.

The brew was good, a batch of Sam Adams I found in McCambridge's. All I needed was an NFL game, shout,

"Go Giants . . ."

and I'd have the US to me.

Without leaning on the metaphor too much, but a drink-fucked PI with mutilated fingers, bad hearing, watching shows that got cancelled — yeah, that's about right.

My phone shrilled. It had that whine that cautioned, *This is nothing good.*

I said,

"Better be good."

Got,

"Taylor, Reardon here."

I took a breath, spat,

"You son of a bitch, you've been Micky Finning me."

Pause.

"Micky what the fuck?"

"Doping me, with some untested shite that could kill me or worse."

He laughed, asked,

"You've been free from hangovers, am I right?"

"At what price, can you tell me that, you bollix?"

More sniggering, then,

"It's life, Jack. We're all fucked."

Maybe we'd been watching the same TV series.

"Jack, you need to rein it in. You'll be suitably rewarded."

"Not in heaven, I hope."

"You're a funny guy, Jack."

"So assholes keep telling me."

"I'll drop by this evening. We can . . . chat."

When I didn't answer, he said,

"One more thing, buddy."

"Yeah?"

"That sense of humour. Keep it honed. You're gonna fucking need it."

He rang off. I cracked another Sam, idled on shooting the bastard the minute he walked in the door. No prelim, no *chat*.

Just blow his shit away.

Made the beer taste even better than it had, gave it an edge.

I was half in the bag when he eventually showed. He was still sporting the grunge look, like a reanimated Cobain:

a pair of combat pants that had designer stains or not,

a T-shirt with the logo *I'd kill for a hit.*

Cute.

He said,

"Yo, bro."

Jesus.

Flopped in the sofa, asked,

"I could go a brew, my man."

I went to the fridge, lobbed a Sam and he caught it expertly. Looked at the label, said,

"Class."

My desire to wallop him had waned as I'd downed enough booze. Normally it fuelled my murderous compulsion, but not this time. I asked,

"This dope you're feeding me. The name . . . is it, like, C for chemical?"

He drained the bottle, belched, said,

"C33?"

"Yeah."

"You don't know?"

He seemed genuinely surprised. I said,

"Like I'd be fucking asking?"

He stood, danced to the fridge, grabbed a brew, flicked the top off, said,

"But, correct me if I'm wrong, you were in the bookstore together, right?"

I was lost, shrugged. He said,

"Kelly. She got the Wilde book that day, I think. Shit, you paid for it, she said."

I stood in front of him, said,

"For fuck's sake, just tell me and quit the fucking riddles."

Unfazed, he said,

"Kelly had a thing for Wilde. C33 is the number of his cell in Reading jail."

Part 2

The Women

29

"*He wanted to be a priest and, at the same time, he was prepared to beat people up and shoot them and kill them. That's not about conflicting goals; that's about The Three Faces of Eve.*"

Edward Dolnick, *The Rescue Artist*

"*Scepticism is the beginning of faith.*"

Oscar Wilde, *The Picture of Dorian Gray*

Ridge was reeling between ferocious grief over Stewart and anger at Jack. Somehow, it had to be Jack's fault, then at least it made some sort of bewildering sense. Jack was nearly always to blame. The whole C33 scenario of Jack's made her boil. Jesus, if there was a conspiracy to be hatched, Jack would be right there, fuelling it. She raged at the cosmic unfairness of it all.

Stewart, who lived so *carefully*. Barely drank, didn't smoke, practised Zen, worked out furiously, and he *dies*. Jack, with his mutilated fingers, near deafness, limp, crazed drinking, intermittent chain-smoking, cocaine binges, diet of every carb known to man, many beatings, flagrant breaking of the law, bad temper, he . . .

He somehow limped on.

She wanted to kill him her own self. Stewart, who supported her in her difficulties with being openly gay, his non-judgemental acceptance of her dead marriage, he was such a blessing. Jack, who fought her tooth and freaking nail over every damn thing, just smirked his way along.

And she was back dwelling on the C33 gig. Was Stewart's murder connected to that? The Guards had his killing down as simply being in the wrong place at the wrong time. In conversation with one of the detectives, she'd been told,

"We'll solve that murder if we get lucky."

Meaning,

We're not putting a whole lot of time and effort there.

The implication,

Stewart had been a dope-dealer,

So . . .

So fuck him.

And was told,

"Leave it alone, won't do your career any good to root around in the dumb death of a dumb fuck."

The tears on her face as she muttered,

"Get a grip, girl."

This stern reprimand brought her father vividly to life. He'd been dead nigh ten years now.

Drink.

Cirrhosis of the liver, not helped by two packs of Major daily. He'd been such a Connemara man, he was almost the fake Irish ideal. Living in the Gaeltacht, he never spoke a word of English and rarely needed to as he refused to venture into what he termed

"Tír na Sasanach."

Land of the English, and that included Galway! He made his living fishing from the legendary Galway Hooker and, like the men of his area, *poitín*. Irish moonshine, brewed from generation to generation until

Ridge.

Yeah, she fucked it up.

And worse, in his eyes, joined the enemy, the bloody *Garda Síochána*. The Guards. Insult to simmering injury. As he lay dying, he'd lashed her with his worst weapon. He refused to speak his native tongue to her, addressed her in halting English, acting like she wouldn't understand her native language. His last words to her, gasped out of an agonized, strangled voice,

"May God forgive thee. I can't and won't."

And died.

Live with that. Perhaps the most enduring curse, the parental one. Of her sexual orientation, he'd rasped to her mother,

"What man would have a turncoat?"

She stood, tried to stem the flow of ferocious memories, all fierce and wounding. Ran her hand along the one shelf of books she'd collected. Jack had been educating her in crime fiction and so far she had seven of the James Lee Burke titles.

And, oh horror, she'd told Jack,

"I'm thinking of getting a Kindle."

Seen him explode.

"Yah dumb bitch, you've read what? Six books, total? And what, you're going to have storage for thousands of books? Get fucking real, lady. You think I'll come round your house, ask, 'Hey, can I browse through your Kindle?'"

Stewart had given her Scott Peck's *People of the Lie* and *The Dummy's Guide to Zen*, which, when she opened it, had nothing but blank pages. Even now, she could clearly see Stewart's smile at his Zen joke.

The Kindle was on hold.

A call from the station: Sharkey, the Super's newest hatchet. Clancy, the boss, liked to take a cop who was a thug to begin with and hone him to effortless viciousness. Sharkey was proving to be the best of the bunch to date, a reptile who'd have shopped his own mother if Clancy asked. He had a quiet voice that held a whiplash of loaded threat. He liked to see the troops dance, dance to a tune they usually didn't understand and daren't contest. Sharkey had, it was said, a long-ago run-in with Jack and lost more than a few teeth. He made it his mission to decimate anyone he saw as Taylor-connected.

Meaning Ridge, big time.

He near whispered,

"Not disturbing anything, I pray."

The slither of his voice like a slow crawl of creepiness. Ridge, to her dismay, stammered, thought *Fuck*.

Said,

"No . . . sir."

A beat,

then,

"No ladies interrupted in flagrante, I trust."

The fuck.

She said,

"Can I be of service . . . sir?"

He gave a snort, then,

"We're rounding up all the deadbeats."

First she thought he meant the public, then realized he meant the cops he despised. Let that stew, then,

"Be here at midnight, we'll tool up."
She wanted to ask,
"What? Tool as in wanker?"
No.
He said,
"Body armour and, trust me, darlin', you're gonna need it." The sneer he injected into *darlin*" was almost artful.

Ice.
What's in a name? The power of TV to shape reality.
To Break Bad — slang for changing from being a citizen to an outlaw.
Crystal meth has the names
Nazi crank,
glass,
ice,
crystal,
or the highly popular *trailer blow*.
It resembles, in its rock form, shards of ice. But comes, too, in
pills,
powder,
and can be
smoked,
injected,
eaten,
snorted.
Supposedly, as in *you hope to fuck*, it bumps
alertness,
energy,

self-esteem,
libido.
Any skel can make it.
Get yourself
fertilizer,
bleach,
a nasal decongestant or three,
a tube, and, oh yeah,
a gas stove,
and if you don't blow the sweet fuck out of your own
self, you're in biz. Welcome to the dope trade.

Now, apart from selling the shit, you've only two
things to focus on:
staying out of jail,
staying alive.
Hear the soundtrack, loud,
"A Town Called Malice",
The Jam,
underwritten always by
The Clash.

Ridge put on the body armour and helmet with the
visor shield, the side pocket of her combat pants
holding pepper spray. The modern version of mother's
little helper. Not quite in the range of the warmth of a
Glock, but, fuck, take what you get.

Sharkey stood before the assembled crew, snapped,
"Listen up."

Like they'd a choice. He ranted,

"The Brennans fancy themselves as the new kids on
the block. The old man, well, someone took a bat to the

geezer, so he's out of the picture, and we have the young blood figuring to play *Game of Thrones*. He is the wee bollix who allegedly may have beat the living shite out of our cherished Sergeant Ridge."

Ripple of smirks and near laughter quelled as Sharkey said,

"But that ain't gonna happen this fine evening, am I right?"

Damn straight.

"Young Brennan got himself a college boy who fancies himself a chemist. They've been brewing up a type of crystal, laced with cough medicine, floor cleaner . . ."

let this sink in,

". . . and, word is, rat poison."

He paused to swig from a flask. It had the crest of Galway United on, and as he swallowed, his face flushed. Ridge figured, *uisce bheatha*, maybe even from her own father's batch. Supplying the Guards had been one of the mainstays of his business.

He continued, fortified,

"Young Brennan got a hard-on with the amount of product they've got, and got a warehouse off the canal, named his version of this lethal crap *Tribe*. A true Galwegian, you might say, save we are going to go fucking Cromwell on his arse, right?"

He was expecting cries of the Marine type.

"Huh! Huh!"

But they were Irish cops, so he got,

"OK."

Not exactly gung-ho, but there it was. Including Sharkey, they numbered seven. Less the magnificent than the mediocre. Sharkey added as they piled into the Black Maria,

"These shitheads have been buying up replica guns, makes them feel like gangstas, and we've had a whisper that a guy in Shantalla adapts those to real fire power. You've been warned."

A young guy, wannabe jarhead with the mandatory buzz cut, Iraq-style pants and desert boots, asked,

"Sarge, how many of these cunts are there?"

Ridge dug him hard in the ribs, said,

"Watch your mouth."

The sergeant said,

"Perhaps six, but who knows? If they're having a *rave*" (Jesus, no one told him how redundant that was) "could be a full deck."

Arriving at the canal, they parked a few yards down from the said warehouse. The top floor of the building was lit up, presumably like the occupants.

They were out of the van, shields ready, a battering ram held by the cess mouth. Up the stairs, and they could hear consternation as the alarm hit. Ridge tried the door. Locked. The ram took it down in two goes.

They were in, pulled on gas masks as three canisters hit the floor, the sarge shouting,

"Everyone down, this is a raid!"

Like, what, they thought it was a gate-crasher?

Ridge could see lines of tables with scientific gear assembled and cauldrons brewing; the cook was in full swing. Guys were attempting to climb out of windows.

268

Batons out, the cops were taking no chances, dropping the party like good 'uns. A young woman, her face streaming from the gas, stood in front of Ridge and levelled a sawed-off. Ridge shouted,

"Don't be freaking daft."

Behind the mask, it sounded like,

"You're flaking gas."

The girl, eyes streaming, muttered,

"Fucking bitch."

And fired.

Ridge had that frozen moment, registered the girl had braces on her teeth. Like that was relevant? Heard, as if in echo,

the Cocteau Twins.

Fucksakes, she hated their music.

Go figure.

And the ice-white clarity of what Stewart must have felt as he faced those lethal barrels.

The gun jammed.

And Ridge's baton was coming up, lashing into the girl's mouth, smashing the braces and the ultra-expensive dental work. A guy beside her yelled,

"Yah stupid cow, this is Mr Westbury's daughter."

Sharkey, beside her, pulling her back, then turning to the guy and kicking him in the balls, said,

"You're nicked, mate."

Back at the station, debriefing done, Ridge was summoned to the Superintendent's office. She was coming off the surge of adrenaline, fear, euphoria, and the realization she could have been killed. Heady stuff, as the posh papers would have it. Clancy's office was packed with cops and a slew of booze lining the desk. A cheer went up as she entered. Clancy moved to her, took her arm, raised it, declared,

"Now this is a Guard!"

She was handed a mug full of Jameson and took a lethal swipe for her nerves. Her eyes watered. Clancy was beaming, his eyes bright with cunning and glee. He said,

"Not only have we brought down a major drug gang, but the shotgun murders are solved. And . . ."

Long pause.

". . . we get to nail the daughter of that fucking showboat Westbury. Girl, you have made us fucking golden."

She wanted to go back at least two sentences and say, "What?"

The shotgun murders. But the gun was never found. Was he saying Westbury's daughter killed Stewart?

It didn't add.

No.

No way.

30

"Purgatory is the country-club prison."

KB

Kelly had tried to replicate the meal as laid out in Joyce's *The Dead*. Like this:

red and yellow jelly,

floury spuds,

figs,

and

Christmas cake.

Some guy had played "The Lass of Aughrim" on, she tried to recall, a harpsichord? Like where the fuck would she get one of those babes?

So she hummed it.

The meal had taken place at

15 Ushers Island

in a house described as *gaunt*.

Well, fucking gaunt she could do. Ask her ex-husbands. She was *doing* Joyce, as she was just a tad peeved at her man, Oscar.

Because Taylor now knew what C33 meant, and worse, who used it. She looked at the time: seven after seven in the evening. Said aloud,

"Presto."

And poured a large seven and seven, because she could, and added,

"Because I'm nuts."

She knew that beyond a shadow, had known for years, and had no problem with it. In fact, if she was pissed about anything, it was that *nuts* was too simplistic. Bundy had told a shrink,

"I'm something new."

As she was.

The books didn't cover her and, God knows, she'd searched, out of a fine sense of interest. When you had a father who was seriously bat shit and *he*, a certifiable lunatic, was afraid of you, well, come on, you've got to be a wee bit curious. By one of those odd quirks, her old man had been confined in the hospital they held Robert Lowell in. It's not the ideal start to a literary obsession, but, hey, it's far more interesting than your Ivy League gig. Lowell, heavily sedated, had seen something *off* in this child, she of the golden locks, enigmatic and fixed smile, had whispered to her,

"Study Wilde."

For years, she thought maybe he'd meant simply,

"Study wild."

As in free and unfettered. But by then it was too late. Some mental osmosis had occurred and, as this coincided with her father's suicide, the die was cast. She'd found her father swinging gently from the oak tree in the garden her mother had so industriously tended. At his feet was *The Collected Oscar Wilde*.

Her inheritance?

Certainly her compass.

Was the child freaked? Depends on how you term that.

She most certainly stood for a long time, staring up at him, "*Daddy*" leaking from her lips, over and over. Not in a hysterical fashion, as in frenzied howling, but more a detached "Look what the cat brung in."

Kind of dawning, as opposed to "Look what the damn cat strung up!"

And a demented soundtrack began in her mind, over:

You are mad. What have I to do with her intrigues with you? Let her remain your mistress. You are well suited to each other. She, corrupt and shameful — you, false as a friend, treacherous as an enemy . . .

When her mother finally appeared and grabbed the child, screaming,

"Oh, Sweet Lord Alabama, what are you muttering, darling?" (her being a child of that there Southern state),

Kelly, cold as ice, said,

"*An Ideal Husband.*"

Her mother looked at her in fear and confusion and Kelly scolded her,

"One does not mutter Wilde, Mother; one intones."

Her father had worked for a large legal firm and was one of the senior partners. Her mother swore the partners drove her husband to suicide to take the rap on serious malpractice allegations. It became a refrain of hers.

"The guilty go free, la di dah."

Followed by the stern command,

"Kelly, make sure someone pays, sometime."

Well, she was trying, kind of.

Kelly took a long time to learn how to disguise who she was. First, she had to find out that it was not considered normal to carry books by Wilde instead of dolls. The fractured connection in her head told her,

Dad keeps dancing with Wilde.

First time she ran this by Mummy, the consterned question,

"What on earth are you muttering?"

Made those early mistakes of trying to explain, as in,

"Daddy was dancing on the rope, he told me that Wilde mattered."

So began the rounds of shrinks — good ones, too. Kelly began to adapt quickly to what these professionals regarded as, if not normal, at least tolerable behaviour. Later, when she read the books and saw the classic signs, like neighbourhood pets disappearing, she knew.

"Leave the fucking pets be."

True, some people disappeared.

Honing her act, Kelly morphed into the all-American girl — blonde, athletic, bouncy, vacant, cloned. On the surface. Only at home did she let her own self out to play.

Caught, once, by Mummy.

Debbi, yes, with the "i", was in the pool, Kelly on the edge, hairdryer poised, and Mummy grabbed her. Kelly, ice even then, warning,

"Careful, Mummy, what if the dryer fell in the pool?"

That evening, they had a talk. Mummy, with a dry Martini, clasped Kelly with *The Duchess of Padua*. A pitcher of Martinis was close to hand. Mummy said,

"I know who you are."

She didn't.

Kelly said,

"Do tell, *Mamma.*"

She went into a long spin about psychosis, personality disorder, malignant spasms, all the while refilling her glass. No stranger to therapy her own self, she had learned the melody without ever knowing the lyrics. Proving that if a little knowledge is a dangerous thing, psychiatric data is deadly. She even delivered, as a *coup de grâce,*

"I've come to the conclusion that you have a narcissistic personality."

Kelly was delighted, said,

"Oh, that is perfect. You, the ultimate in vanity, dare to even utter such . . .

such . . ."

She truly had to reach for a word, settled for,

"Horseshit."

Then without missing a beat, intoned,

"*And if he does not drink it,*

Why, then they will kill him."

Smiled beatifically at her mother, said,

"From *The Duchess of Padua.*"

Her mother stared at her drink in dawning horror, asked,

"Did . . . did you put something in my glass?"

Kelly, with another beatific smile, said,

"Of course."

A beat.

"Ice."

31

"*Let's face it. If I wasn't as talented as I am ambitious, I'd be a gross monstrosity.*"

Madonna

Reardon was the original bad boy. But smart, way, way smart. His true cleverness lay in finding people of near genius and getting them to work for him. Kelly was studying psychology at Kent and met Reardon on the very day he'd been expelled. He was heading out, his thumb out, and she'd stopped in her flash new Corvette.

Why?

Because she liked to play and he had a built-in smirk. Like,

"Gimme a ride, or not. Who gives a fuck?"

Her kind of thinking. He threw a battered duffel in the car, slid in, lit up a spliff, said,

"If you're a cop, I'm way fucked."

She studied him, asked,

"And you care?"

He slipped on a pair of ultra-expensive shades (she knew, as she'd stolen similar), then he looked at her, said,

"Thing is, I got bounced from college today. Another bust would be . . ."

blew out smoke,

". . . a bummer."

That was how they began.

As she would discover over and over, Reardon *knew a guy* who'd invented an early version of the easy-fit seal that kept refrigeration turning. Reardon knew enough to go in partnership fifty-fifty, then peddled the seal to the army. And got, he said,

"The first easy billion."

He was a year older than Kelly and, on his twenty-first, they got married in Venice — the one in Europe. Reardon was, of course, persuading the EU how much they needed an early form of the iPad for translators. The night he clinched the deal, he told her,

"How much for you to fuck off?"

And she'd laughed, actually came as close to loving him as was possible. They'd reached if not peace, then a perverse understanding. He knew she was mired in some darkness but felt no compulsion to investigate. At some deep level, he knew she *had his back*, and that was plenty. In the lethal deals he was involved in, and the plans he had for the future, a family ally was gold.

They neither dissolved nor advertised their marriage.

It was what it was.

I'd tried to find Kelly, but she'd gone to ground. I phoned Reardon, who said,

"You're asking me?"

Well, yeah.

Said,

"Aren't you her some kind of half-arsed husband?"

He laughed, said,

"All the more reason I've no clue where she is."

I said,

"And sounds like you could give a fuck."

A pause.

"Taylor, best not to be a smart mouth to me. I mean, at best, I tolerate you. You have some vague uses, but don't think you have an *in* to a single fucking thing that goes on in my personal life."

I said,

"Touchy."

Long sigh from him. It's been my life that, sooner or later, most I know get to sigh. Like some warped theme tune to my mad existence.

He said,

"Taylor, you've got some cock-eyed notion that C33, so named by Kelly, gives you a clue to the bizarre killings that happened. Take this on trust, *caballero*, even if by some wild stretch you could link Kelly to any of this crap, you do not, definitely do not, want to have her put you in her gun sights."

I laughed, kind of, said,

"Gee, sounds like some kind of threat."

Heard him mutter to someone, then,

"One thing Kelly and I still retain from our marriage . . ."

Bitterness leaking over me, I shot,

"Yeah? Like fucking people over?"

"We don't threaten."

Pause.

"We deliver."

Rang off.

It's always been my lot to be easily distracted, to be turned aside from the case before me. I believe it's a blend of denial, cussedness, cowardice and sheer disinterest. Plus side trips along the roads of

alcoholism,

Xanax,

books,

and, very rarely,

a woman.

I don't know what I think I ought to know, but fuck, I know my own act, and it is a cocktail of sordid self-interest, self-doubt and, of course, self-harm. That doesn't make me bad so much as Irish. I fully intended focusing on Kelly, her connection to the C33 killings, but

hurling.

The All-Ireland final.

Between Galway and the maestros, Kilkenny. Christ, those cats are good. Galway hadn't won the title in twenty-four years so we were, like,

due.

The town was electric, wired even more than when the Volvo Ocean Race had its conclusion in our docks. The city was hopping, drinking and anticipatory. Flags everywhere.

A draw.

A fucking draw.

Jesus, everyone hates that. You've to go through all the same crap again, like Tom Russell sang,

"*And go through all that shit again.*

Precisely."

We'd to wait three weeks with the pundits analysing why the underdog (us) usually won on the rebound, as it were.

We didn't.

Three fucking points and we were done for another year. Did we take it badly?

You fucking betcha.

Guy said to me,

"Great thing is, they are a young team, we've got time."

What about me? Time? I can barely draw me breath.

My mobile shrilled. I snapped it up, rasped,

"Yeah?"

Heard a cultured voice.

"Hell of a way to answer your phone."

The voice familiar but escaping me. I pushed,

"So?"

"This is Mr Westbury, legal eagle."

Fuck's sake, *Mister*. They call themselves that and you can translate: *prick*.

Asked,

"Can I help you?"

He chuckled, then,

"It's actually what I'm going to do for you."

I sneered,

"Gee, I kind of doubt that."

He wasn't fazed, continued,

"Your buddy Stewart left a will."

"You're shitting me."

Another chuckle, though of the incredulous variety. He said,

"What a turn of phrase you have. Have you ever considered writing? They tell me mystery is the money-spinner these days, and Lord knows, you talk in a disjointed fashion that might even pass for style."

Hilary Mantel had just won the Booker for the second time with, would you believe,

Bringing Up the Bodies.

Serendipity?

The fuck cares.

I asked,

"Surely Stewart was too young to have made a will?"

He tut-tutted.

I swear to God.

That an adult can actually do this is a source of constant astonishment to me. He said,

"Stewart was a conscientious young man and a shrewd entrepreneur. One feels making such a wise move would not have been a choice of yours, Mr Taylor."

Bollix.

I said,

"It's the dilemma of who to leave my Zippo to that's held me back."

"Very droll, I'm sure."

I said,

"Much as I love kibitzing with you, is there a point?"

"Indeed. Stewart left you a considerable sum."

I muttered,

"Jesus H. Really?"

He said, in the dryest tone,

"Would I be . . . *shitting* you?"

★ ★ ★

En route to Westbury's office, I walked along Shop Street, the buskers and mimes in full and silent roar, respectively. One was attracting a lot of attention, made up like Mitt Romney. He'd a sign around his neck which read,

I pledge to nuke Iran.

One felt he'd keep his awful promise.

A band was playing "The Fields of Athenry", and for any decent Irish person the song has resonance, but when it's their sole repertoire and you've heard it for the tenth time, you're prepared to lay waste the bloody fields. I was not alone in my thinking. The government was introducing legislation that required buskers to have, I kid you not, at least twenty songs!

Like, who the fuck was going to enforce this? Some lone dumb Guard would have to stand there and, like, hear twenty awful Irish ballads.

He'd run screaming for duty in the Lebanon.

Then I did a double-take. Was I finally succumbing to all my excesses and hallucinating in broad daylight? I saw

a Segway.

Those stand-up, slow mobile things that somebody thought were a grand idea. A lone Guard, self-conscious and mortified, was . . . cruising? . . . along by Griffin's bakery to jeers and mockery from just about everyone, even, God help us, tourists.

The Guard said,

"Those are to be the latest weapon in the war against street crime."

I mean, fucking seriously.

The street thugs are carrying everything from freaking Uzis to grenades and this lone eejit on his trusty Segway appears and does what? Shouts,

"Halt, or I shall pursue."

Jesus.

A woman, not young, was outside Boots, singing "One Day at a Time".

But almost inaudibly until she hit the refrain, of "Lord Help Me Jesus".

And man, she hit that sucker with all she'd got.

This was, collectively, Dante's Irish edition of the Seventh Circle.

I got that sudden thirst that knows nought of rhyme nor race, stepped into Garavan's. The owner was there, a good guy. He knew to leave you be until you got the first drink down.

He offered the *Irish Independent* with the pint; news and stout, the staples. Got half the black away and sat back, wished for a smoke and, I swear, the guy beside me asked,

"Wanna fag?"

Not a question you'd ask an American.

I'd been, yet again, on,

then off,

and yada yada.

But, what the hell. I said,

"Yeah."

We didn't go to the smokers' shed — too much like a leper colony — but took it out on the street. He offered a pack of Major, the original ferocious-strength one. He produced a battered Zippo, clicked. One of my favourite sounds. Fired us up.

Jesus, that pure poison is pure heaven. The guy was in his early twenties, dressed in good top-of-the-range clothes. His face had that ravaged look of hellish teenage acne, but he had good eyes, those gentle ones you see rare to rarest in either a child or a Labrador, a sort of beguiling innocence. He said,

"I was thinking of going to Australia."

The sarcasm in me nearly said,

"Finish the fag first."

But I bit down, said,

"Lots of work there."

We'd fallen instantly into the camaraderie of smokers. He said,

"My girl, you know, she's a nurse, she doesn't want to leave Galway."

Jesus, why not, to live in the sun, where the buskers might play another tune?

I said,

"Tough choice."

He drew deep on the filter, then,

"What's tough is she's reading *Fifty Shades of Grey*."

Is there a sane reply?

Berryman in the *Paris Review*:

"the artist is extremely lucky who is presented with the worst possible ordeal which will not actually kill him. At that point he's in business."

I'd finished my pint, forwent another or I'd be there until closing, and headed for Westbury's office.

Kept me waiting an hour, old *Reader's Digests* on the table. I increased my word power by two.

Butyraceous: of the nature or consistency of butter.

Caesious: bluish or greenish grey.

Not sure how to drop those babes into conversation.

When I finally got to sit opposite Westbury, his fabulously expensive suit was the colour of . . .

Caesious?

And, certainly, fine food, lots of the best wine, had given his jowls a butyraceous sheen.

He shuffled papers in that important fashion they must teach at law school. He was peering over his pince-nez (made me feel warm and literary to call it that instead of glasses), his expression sour, as if I was something the cat not only snuck in but then denied.

He said,

"You'll find all is in order, and may I say congrats on your little windfall."

He passed me over some papers. I scanned them, then said,

"Holy fuck."

It was a lot.

He asked,

"Might you be needing some expert advice on how best to manage those substantial assets?"

I laughed, let out,

"Like fuck."

He said,

"One takes that as a no."

32

"I'm allergic to alcohol and narcotics. I break out in jail."

Robert Downey, Jr

In my mind, it was Peter O'Toole as Lawrence of Arabia saying,

"The trick is not minding that it hurts."

Didn't work on thinking about Stewart.

A guy passed me wearing a T with the logo,

BEST BOY BAND — ONE ERECTION.

I was meeting Ridge to have a drink to say a final goodbye to Stewart, now that his estate was settled. We met in Feeney's, at the top of Quay Street. It's somehow hung on as a real pub, if not indeed ordinary because they don't serve chips.

Yet.

Fishing tackle was advertised in a front window alongside Middleton Whiskey. A lone sentry sat at the end of the bar. If he remembered me, he didn't let on. His flat cap was on the counter, lined up beside a dwindling pint. I offered,

"Another?"

Took my measure, then,

"Will I have to thank you?"

"Good heavens, no."

He nodded.

No change there.

I sat near the back, a short and a tabloid before me. The sublime and the scurrilous. I was reading about the American election when Ridge appeared. Her face looked ravaged, like a continuous jag of weeping. I didn't ask, offered,

"Something to drink?"

Surprised me with,

"A hot toddy."

As I moved to get it, she added,

"Make it a large."

Indeed.

The barman didn't ask if cloves were required or what whiskey. It was old Galway, so cloves and Jameson as sure as the swans were in the Claddagh basin. Smelled so good, I ordered one my own self. Brought them back and she wrapped her hands round the glass, hot as it was, like a forlorn rosary, said,

"Stewart left me a shit pile of money."

"Me, too."

She seemed surprised, but not enough to compare figures. She took a gulp of the drink, swallowed, and shuddered as the whiskey hit. Her face turned a bright high-proof red, her eyes watered and she was temporarily robbed of speech.

Why we drink the stuff.

Finally, she said,

"I'm giving the money away."

Ah, for fooksakes, Jesus. I waited a beat, asked,

"Why?"

294

Trying not to let bitterness leak over my tone. She seemed not to notice, said,

"My neighbour, Kathleen, used to go every evening for cat food, five o'clock."

This abrupt turn in the conversation didn't faze me. Put it down to the Jay. I said,

"Did she?"

Her glass was empty, and bearing in mind it was a double, I hesitated before offering another. She said,

"Kathleen didn't have a cat."

I had to roll with it, gave a brief smile as if it made some sense. She continued,

"She'd go to Dunne's, buy half a bottle of vodka and drink it on the way home."

This insanity made bizarre sense to me, but, then, I'd been drinking in a lunatic fashion for so long that the only thing to surprise me would be social drinking.

The aim of life is self-development. To realize one's nature perfectly.

Kelly felt she'd followed Oscar's dictum pretty closely. Now, as she lay flat on the table, the guy leaned over her back, glanced at the portrait she'd provided, asked,

"Who is the dude? Is it, like, Rupert Everett?"

She laughed, as indeed the actor had played Oscar, and quite convincingly. She said,

"Can you do it?"

He moved the needle back, said,

"Babe, you got the cash, I can put the Rolling Stones on there."

As if.

The guy had offered, as he put it,

"A spliff, or something to, you know, ease the pain?"

For Oscar, pain was bliss and she wanted to *feel* him.

The guy worked in silence, then asked,

"Mind if I take a cig break?"

She sat up, not covering her breasts, but the guy didn't stare. He rolled a Taylor-made, lit up, sighed, said,

"That's gonna cover your whole back, you know?"

She waited. The Stieg Larsson gig was due to come around.

Yup.

He said,

"Like *The Girl with the Dragon Tattoo*."

So she said,

"Who'd you prefer, Noomi Rapace or the Hollywood chick?"

Leaning on *chick* just to, you know, like fuck with him. He said,

"I don't do flicks."

Took her a moment to realize he meant movies, so she said,

"Whatever."

A guy came bursting in, big fellah in a biker jacket, red face, eyes popping, like meth jag or something, shouted,

"Who the fuck owns the grey BMW?"

She looked at him, said in a meek tone,

"That'd be me."

He glared at her, snarled,

"Yah stupid cunt."

For some time, she'd felt herself disintegrating, had read about the effect in countless books, but couldn't believe it would take her.

It was and it did.

She shot a hand out, grabbed the tattoo needle and jammed it in the guy's eye, said,

"Language."

The tattoo guy stared in horror as the man roared, the needle vibrating in the socket, and it seemed like for ever before he fell to the floor. Kelly put her shirt on, put some money on the table, said,

"We'll pick this up later."

Thinking,

Fuck, I'm forgetting something.

As she drove off, she remembered,

Don't leave witnesses.

But mostly she felt sadness that only part of Oscar covered her back. That made her laugh and she shouted,

"Who's got my back, eh? Answer me that."

The BMW stalled at a traffic light. She heard the constant whine of Reardon, if not of reason,

Godammit, you're flooding the engine.

A young guy, maybe seventeen, whistled,

at her,

the car,

the stalling,

or a combo,

wasn't clear.

She rolled down the window, asked,

"Want this car?"

He did a double-take, went,

"You're fookin' jokin'?"

She got out, handed him the keys, said,

"Go for it."

He took the keys, slid in tentatively, asked,

"What's the catch?"

She smiled, said,

"Only one requirement."

He'd already decided to get like double fuck time out of there, but played, said,

"Yeah?"

"Be Meatloaf."

"Wha'?"

"Like a bat out of hell."

He did.

Tyres screeching, no flooded engine now. She thought,

What would Oscar do?

A cocktail.

But of course.

The Skef was running a Happy Hour. She perched on the long bar, asked the sharp-looking bar guy,

"You do Long Island Tea?"

"Does Greece long for the drachma?"

That being a yes.

Showed he was not only a graduate of handsome lessons but down with, like, events, as in current.

He served the drink with a flourish. She hoped to fuck he wouldn't say,

"*Voilà*."

He did.

She tasted it, said,

"Mmmm,"

asked,

"You ever see *Basic Instinct?*"

No.

The guy wasn't the brightest, so she spelled it out.

"Wanna fuck?"

In the bathroom, as they tore each other's clothes off, he stopped, gasped,

"Your back . . . it's bleeding!"

She adopted a Brit accent, went,

"It's bleeding Oscar."

I'd just woken up, barely had the shower and stuff done, was about to have the first kick-ass coffee, when the doorbell went.

Loud and insistent.

I muttered,

"Fuck."

Pulled it open to Ridge and another Guard, both in pressed uniforms. I snapped,

"What?"

Needed to be on the second cup of caffeine before I could listen to whatever shite they brought. It was never good and always way too early. Ridge said,

"Let's take this inside."

We did.

Ridge, glancing around, not seeing anything to warm her, asked,

"Are you alone?"

I grabbed my cup, got some down, asked,

"You mean in the metaphysical sense?"

The other Guard, young and obviously gung-ho, eager to test his power, commanded,

"Answer the question."

I looked at him. Ah, to be twenty-two and stupid. I asked,

"Or what?"

Ridge, flexing her sergeant's stripe, said,

"Yesterday your lady friend stabbed a man to death."

I knew, I fucking knew, it could only be one person. Stalled.

"Need a little more than that."

She could play, said,

"Kelly Reardon."

I finished the coffee, waited for the kick, said,

"I haven't seen her."

The young guard looked round, like he'd like to be sure. Ridge sighed, said,

"If you do hear from her, I trust you'll be in touch."

I gave her my best smile, said,

"Trust — loaded word."

She let that slide, said,

"Later."

Headed out.

The young cop lingered. I'd an idea of what was coming. He said,

"Heard you were a Guard."

I smiled, said,

"This is where you tell me that won't cut me any slack, and oh, yeah, in a measured tone you'll tell me you don't like me."

He reddened — even younger than I thought. I continued,

"You see, for it to matter that *you* don't like someone, *you* have to matter, and trust an old Guard on this, you are a long way from mattering to anyone, so hustle back to Toytown."

And slammed the door on him.

Another enlistment in the ranks of those who loathed me.

Fun though.

The coffee was way cold. Was it too early for a Jay? Not if the cops have been, so maybe a wee dram. Sat in an armchair, tried to figure out about Kelly obviously unravelling. No doubt in my mind now: she was the vigilante killer and, more than likely, Stewart's killer, too. What was I going to do now in light of my feelings for her?

The Jay answered that.

"Kill the bitch."

I broke into Reardon's house.

Why?

Because I could.

Five in the afternoon and the winter darkness had already settled. The house was lit up like hope. I knew sensor alarms were to be installed in the grounds but, due to a strike with the grounds staff, it was in limbo. And, yes, I did say *grounds staff.*

No point in being sick rich if you didn't flaunt it.
Like,

two gardeners,

security guards,

gamekeeper (I shit thee not),

and all attending a Galway United match. Thank
fuck. Reardon his own self was the guest of honour at
the match. I figured on somebody being home but was
intending to avoid them. I mostly hoped Kelly would
be there. I was carrying

nine mil.

I'd a scenario in my head. See her and just pump two
in her fucking head, no frills.

A kitchen window was fairly easily manoeuvred. The
alarm it should have set off was, like the rest, at the
match. God bless football. I stood in the kitchen,
listened. Quiet. Lights were on all over but I felt they
were cosmetic. The house felt empty. Nevertheless, I let
the nine slide to my right hand, headed for the stairs,
stopped en route, had a glass of rye — keep it US.
Tasted good, tasted like I wanted more. I moved on up
the stairs, did a full search of six bedrooms, not a
dickey bird.

So, OK.

I'd wait.

Back downstairs, another rye, with ice; just because I
felt like fucking with my own head, I sat in a large
leather chair, settled in. The room had a comfortable
feel, lots of books that had never been opened. I know
my used books. When books are for show, be sure
you've put ammunition in the nine, double check.

It was close to midnight when the front door opened. I'd turned the lights down so it appeared undisturbed. Reardon's voice and a woman laughing.

Kelly.

Shoot them both?

It wasn't Kelly. They'd walked into the living room, arm in arm, she still laughing at something he'd said. I did recognize her, vaguely, from a recent reality show that was like all those shows, about fucking nothing. Worse, nothing with what they thought of as *street cred*.

Jesus.

She had one of those new bogus Irish names, like

Blaitín

or

Sneachta.

Which translate as *flowers* and *snow*, respectively. I don't know either. Their sole function seems to be the annoyance factor. I had the gun down by my leg and felt there was little need to show it now. Reardon reacted smartly, said,

"Jack, glad you could come by."

I went with,

"Sorry to intrude, but I felt it was best to report personally."

The woman was pissed, whined,

"You're working *now*?"

Man, she sure leaned on that *now*. Managing a world of complaint in it. Seriously, I don't think anyone would ever call what Reardon did *work*, but, hey, she was a reality star. But he liked to play, always, said,

"Jack's my gopher, you know, the one who jumps when I whistle."

Building a whole amount of sneer into that. She liked it, pushed,

"Get him to jump now."

Maybe I'd just shoot her.

A long moment. We were frozen in a tableau of dislike. Reardon broke the spell, said,

"Jack has to run along now. Isn't that right, Jack? There's a good boy, hop it."

The sneer was so inbuilt, you could almost miss it — almost. I stood, slipping the nine into the pocket of Item 1834, my all-weather Garda coat, asked,

"Any idea of where your wife might be?"

The reality genius heard wrong, laughed, said,

"Is he looking for a wife, Daniel?"

Daniel. Jesus, who knew?

I'd of course read about Danny Reardon, American poet / actor / author who now lectured at Trinity, but, I figured, no kin. Daniel smiled.

"Jack, you're a PI and asking me?"

The bright spark was about to ask something and he lashed her, fast, with,

"Shut . . . the . . . fuck . . . up."

She did.

I looked right into his eyes, let him see I was not fucking around, said,

"Best for all if maybe I find her before, you know, the cops?"

We both knew that was a crock. He asked,

"Where would Oscar flee to?"

I was on my way out, a slight tremor niggling at my nerve ends. I heard, in whine song,

"Who's Oscar?"

Galway was on the world stage for all the wrong worst reasons.

An Indian woman died of blood poisoning after being denied a pregnancy termination. Though she was in severe pain, the hospital refused to act as they said there was still a foetal heartbeat and this was a Catholic country.

Previously, she'd been told she was having a spontaneous abortion and the foetus had no chance. Details of the woman's horrendous agony and agonizing death led to immediate street protests, and crowds from both sides of the abortion divide shouted at each other outside the hospital.

The government ducked and dived, muttering platitudes, adding fuel to the notion that they were the most hated government we'd ever had. The new austerity measures, seemingly more of them daily, had the people already at breaking point.

I was in Garavan's, a pint before me, and a man in a splendid suit, with groomed hair, a tan, knocked back a large gin and tonic and pronounced,

"See, say what the fuck you like, the Church still rules this country. The clergy might have a lower profile but they are still covert. Abortion is their ticket back."

His use of the obscenity seemed especially offensive. A photo of the deceased woman was on all the front pages. She had one of those lovely faces that testified to a gentle soul. The suit turned to me, assessed me, found me wanting, asked — demanded,

"What do you think, fellah?"

I moved from my stool, looked at him, said,

"You shout the odds in a pub, but what are you going to do?"

This seemed to baffle him. He echoed,

"Do? What can I *possibly* do?"

I hadn't the energy to start, said,

"Gotcha."

He grabbed my arm, hissed,

"What's that mean, eh? We're a nation of talkers, we shout and rant, it's our heritage."

"But what happened to the country of fighters?" I asked.

"Not the point," he said.

More's the Irish pity.

33

"Naturally," he said, "I don't defend evil deeds, but if you can't understand the nature of crime . . . the motives of a criminal . . . well, you won't get very far as a detective. There is a sort of twisted logic which is often easier to discover than the logic which governs our everyday actions. As we all know, chaos is the neighbour of God; but everything's usually neat and tidy in hell . . ."

Hakan Nasser, *Hour of the Wolf*

Finally did a detective thing — found the apartment Kelly lived in when she wasn't staying at Reardon's place. Knew she had to have a separate territory.

How?

I asked the ESB.

Light bills have caught more villains than the Guards.

The apartment was in Devon Park, formerly a rich enclave. The whole of the bottom floor was in her name. I had a clipboard and a puzzled expression, basically the only tools essential for burglary. Those and a bent key. I got in without triggering alarms. My second break-in in a week, it struck me — maybe a whole new line of work.

The living room was spotless, I mean vacuumed to an inch of its fibre. Leather easy chairs and a large lived-in sofa.

One massive bookcase.

Wilde.

As in hundreds of Oscar volumes. A top shelf devoted to true crime and psychology.

Ann Rule.

People of the Lie.

Books on Bundy and all the boyos. But most telling, a three-volume *Study on Women Psychopaths and Sociopaths*.

One volume seemed to be especially well-thumbed so I took that. And must have triggered something in the shelf as suddenly all the lights came on, the radio, the huge-screen TV. Put the shite crossways in me. I literally jumped. Moved quickly around, turned off everything save the TV.

I found the drinks cabinet, and phew-oh, a veritable wet dream for an alky. I settled for a fine old single malt. The TV was tuned to Setanta, our version of ESPN.

Showing Sweden *vs*. England and Ibrahimovic's spectacular scissor goal. It was in a loop play and I watched, mesmerized, as:

1. he focused on the ball, bent his knees to prepare,
2. the non-kicking left foot leaves the ground first,
3. the left foot's rapid upward swing gets him airborne,
4. in mid air! . . . he brings the kicking boot into play,
5. the right foot strikes the ball in a looping goal-aimed trajectory,
6. the sheer power, rush of the strike, somersaults his body as he then lands on his feet to punch the air.

He knew that baby was going to goal.

"Jesus," I muttered, "what a thing of beauty."

I checked the bedroom: neat, tidy, brand-new clothes still in their wrappers. Ten pairs of expensive shoes

310

lined up, and I knew the price as the tags were still intact. A Michael Mortell coat on the door peg, also unworn. I stepped back, thought,

A life waiting to be lived, truly on hold, but for what?

Bathroom. Usually a treasure of medication, you can at least hope for a slew of valium. Nope, just a bottle of Joop!

Jesus — with the tag *Real men wear pink*. Surely an Oscar link. If you ignored the bookcase, there was nothing to say anyone lived here. This was vacancy writ large to largest.

I'd learned absolutely fuck all. I took one final sweep through, not even sure what I hoped to find. In the kitchen, on top of the fridge, was a TV guide and I flicked the pages.

One series heavily underlined.

The Booth at the End.

Of the myriad things I longed to share with Stewart, discuss, fight over, this series was prime. Begun as a twenty-minute internet sensation, now a five-part series directed by Adam Arkin, it was *The Twilight Zone* meets *The Zen of the Diner*.

It was punk, street metaphysics, and I no longer could watch it as every line I wanted to shout,

"Stewart, get a load of this."

Fuck to fucked loss.

Why she'd that marked didn't provide a whole lot more light. The bitch was a stone-cold psycho, unravelling faster than a propeller cycle backward kick. I sat on a hard cane chair, put my head in my hands

311

and wondered when the grief would ebb. I mused on the five stages of grief they extol and said,

"Hey, I took the shortcut, rage to outright violence."

The nine was in my jacket and I withdrew it, shot the fridge four times. Childish, indeed, but, you know, it felt better to actually let rip.

Got ready to leave, stared at the now dripping fridge, muttered,

"Soul on ice."

I met a woman outside, elderly, not carrying rosary beads but had the look. She asked,

"Did you hear . . . shots?"

I said,

"Only the one heard round the world, but that wasn't recent."

Asking myself,

"Where would Oscar go?"

Not London. Not after they'd jailed him. Paris? Hmmm . . . He'd lived on

the fake and humiliating kindness of strangers.

Italy?

I'd need to check that out.

I was standing on the Salmon Weir Bridge, where the salmon no longer leaped, the water still, five years on, poisoned. Like the fucking country. The cathedral to my left, noon Mass letting out, and sparse — not too many attending these days. A forlorn priest outside, shaking the hands of the measly faithful, grateful they weren't, I suppose, a lynch mob.

I turned my back on them, headed to town, stopped in the Cellar; used to be the student joint. But they, like everyone else, were getting take-outs, bringing it on back home. Cider and Red Bull, instant wasted, from A to out of your fucking head in jig time. The Cellar had a flash coffee dock, with even a *barista*.

You've truly lived too long when an Irish guy, in a mock mid-Atlantic accent, asks,

"How would you like your java, sir?"

Way too tempting a question to answer truthfully. The bar was way too flash, too brightly lit. No hiding of blemishes here, every dark mark of my existence on neon.

About to turn when a guy sitting on a stool went,

"Jack?"

Took me a second, then . . . Tremlin — joined the force just as I was about to get my arse handed to me. Had run into him a few times. Not the worst, which in Ireland is a huge compliment. He liked his pint, so he couldn't be all rotten. I moved back, shook his large calloused hand, like a man who'd tilled fields — and recently. I recalled he'd a rep as a brawler. An essential if increasingly discreet part of most police forces. He asked,

"Buy you a jar?"

"Great."

The barman, obviously related to the *barista*, judging by his fake tan and delicately tied ponytail, asked,

"Like to try the new concoction?"

Fuck.

Concoction.

The pubs I frequented, that word usually came with a phone warning, going,

"You have five minutes to clear the premises."

I asked,

"What is it?"

"Lager and Guinness blended."

"Holy fuck, you're kidding."

He wasn't.

We'd got past, somehow, that we no longer owned our national beverage, even tried to forget the whole Guinness-Lite nonsense, and let's never mention the White Guinness, but with Lager?

Fucksake.

He did manage to pour a half-decent pint and Tremlin and I took our drinks to a table. He sighed, said,

"God be with the days we could smoke."

In a spirit of misguided camaraderie, I joked,

"And beat the bejaysus out of the public."

Phew-oh, that sank.

Cloud of utter darkness flitted across his features. I could sense his whole body tense. I lied quickly, added,

"You're looking fit, my man."

Lame, huh?

He downed his shot and I signalled for another. I tried,

"Not your usual pub, this?"

He gave me a long look, then,

"Nothing is usual no more."

He managed to include the whole of life's rich tapestry in this. The drinks came. I handed the guy a twenty, wondering if in these days of *baristas* that even covered one drink. Tremlin hugged the glass with both hands, said,

"Your girl is making waves."

Threw me.

Kelly?

Nope.

He continued.

"She was responsible for that major drug gig, you know, got some serious points there."

I nodded, implying *a good 'un indeed*, then he added, as if it was a throwaway,

"Pity she's a fucking lezzie."

As I took a moment to grasp this casual slice of icy bigotry, he knocked back his drink, said,

"My daughter, Oonagh, she finished college and, like every other young wan, looks like she'll have to emigrate, so I was wondering . . ."

Let his wonder hang there, like a sad dead prayer.

I asked,

"What?"

He fidgeted, took a whiskey breath, said,

"If you'd . . . ask Mr Reardon. She's a great girl, real go-getter, he wouldn't regret it."

Fuck.

I asked,

"Reardon? Why would you think he'd listen to me?"

He gave a sly smile, ugly in its nicotine blemish, said,

"You're his go-boy. Jesus, no shame in that, we all have to eat some shite, right? Am I right, boyo?"

Go boy.

Count the ways I was phrasing to tell him to fuck his own self when he said,

"'Course, no one eats for free, right, Jack-o? So I could put some info your way, as a . . . sweetener."

For once, I bit down, said nothing, waited.

He looked round, as if the pub was hanging on our every golden word, then,

"I know where the cunt is."

You had to admit, the guy had new ways of using the language to foul and besmirch. I stared at him and he said,

"The American nutter, I know where she went."

Least I figured his toilet mouth had wound down and I asked,

"Why would I want to know?"

He said, staring me right in the eye,

"Sure, the whole town knows you were riding the bitch."

34

"Manson was a crazy fuck, tipsy with demons which paced him a degree higher than Nick Copeland because Nick had everything to live for, had put his family first (so had Manson, well, in a way) and Nick had failed without even a hint of notoriety."

J. P. Smith, *Airtight*

Prince Paul: "I would much sooner talk scandal in a drawing room than treason in a cellar."

Oscar Wilde, Vera

Time ago, in *The Killing of the Tinkers*, a former priest said to me, bitterness leaking over every measured word,

"Jack, a terrible darkness is hovering. It's going to be the passing of the priests, where once they trod on hallowed ground, now they will tread on the thinnest ice. Lunch parties will be replaced by lynch ones. To wear the roman collar will be to wear a bull's-eye on their back."

I'd had a few, the Jay sinking nicely, whispering nice warm lies to me, and I trivialized his prophecy, said,

"Ary, go on our' that, they will always pull off the ecclesiastical smoke and mirrors."

He'd stared into a dwindling pint of the black, seeing nothing but demons, howling ones, said,

"You will see not so much the end of days but a rise in such as

Scientology,

the Black Arts,

sham clairvoyants,

fundamentalism."

He'd stood abruptly, shot out of the pub. And in those days I cared enough to follow him. He was huddled in a doorway, gulping down a cigarette as if it were Holy Communion. He coughed and I asked him,

"What will *you* do?"

He gave me a look of utter surprise, as if the thought had never occurred to him, said,

"I'm going the Irish way."

I mused on that, then tried,

"Pretend it isn't happening, or, worse, confined to the UK."

He laughed, no relation to joy or humour, said,

"I'll slow-drink myself to oblivion."

I made light, said,

"I doubt that."

He nodded, crushed the butt into the ground with vehemence, said,

"You're right. Scratch the *slow* shite."

Call it serendipity or just sheer shite bad luck. That priest was running through my mind,

for reasons

not at all,

when I heard,

"Taylor!"

in that tone of

Get over here . . . now!

Imperative, very.

I was on Shop Street, just outside Tommy Hilfiger, who, despite the so-called pestilence of recession, was doing a roaring trade.

Go figure.

★ ★ ★

The bane of my life has been a friend of my late mother. Her very own tame priest, he was easier to maintain than a dog and cheaper to feed; he simply needed pious platitudes as a rudimentary diet. Her part of the deal was to look good with a priest in tow. These changed days, you'd be safer to tow a rabid Rottweiler, and considerably safer. Father Malachy.

Phew-oh.

What a charged lethal history we had.

He loathed, despised and downright hated me. Straight up.

And get this for Irish irony: I saved the bollix's hide, and was he grateful?

Was he by fuck.

Few more resentful than those you've helped. The gas part was, he hated priests more than most. His *calling* was a joke. It was purely a job and one he detested. Said to me once,

"Confessions — fuckers whining about beating wives and getting drunk. I should be so lucky."

He was dressed in the priestly gear rare to rarest these days, due to the suspected public fatwa, his suit jacket a riot of either dandruff or ash, or both. His pockets bulging like a cheeky boy who'd raided an orchard, save he carried many packs of cigs and

lighter,

matches,

handkerchief,

nasal spray,

breath freshener.

Well, maybe the last one not so much, but one could hope. He looked diminished, not just by age and nicotine. A year back he'd been set on by a vile gang named Headstone and had never quite recovered.

Who would?

It saddened me, no matter how much I despised him, and I did, but it was no joy to see him fade. He was a tangible link to my past and a reminder, too, that once I'd held belief. He stared at me, said,

"Jaysus, you look like something the dog refused to drag in."

I smiled, glad of the constant.

Then he asked,

"Would you come for a drink?"

By all that's unholy, it was startling. Next, he might even offer to pay, but that would be stretching it. I said,

"Sure, where'd you have in mind?"

He gave a sly grin.

"Someplace you're not barred."

We went to Richardson's on the Square, still family-run, by some amazing miracle. The barman said,

"Good day to you, Father."

And got,

"What's bloody good about it? Bring us a couple pints and slow draw them."

The barman wasn't fazed. Like I said, a family place.

We sat in the corner, Malachy with his back to the wall, eyeing the door. Beatings do that. A light sweat broke out on his forehead and I recognized the onset of a panic attack. I said,

"Take a deep breath."

He snarled,

"Take a fucking jump in the Corrib."

He tore off his jacket, let it fall to the floor, and when I went to retrieve it he snapped,

"Leave it."

My sadness for him was eroding fast.

The pints came, I toasted,

"*Sláinte.*"

He spat,

"Bad cess to them all."

Them being an Irish generic term for all the gobshites who crossed his path in vexation. He killed that pint like a nun on ecclesiastical meth, wiped his mouth, said,

"I'm off for a fag."

He was rooting in his jacket when he noticed I wasn't moving, asked,

"Aren't yah coming?"

I said, quite demurely I thought,

"I don't do that type of thing any more."

My tone framed for max annoyance.

Landed.

He said,

"Jaysus, the day you give up anything, there's a new wing in Hell."

And off he stomped.

A book had fallen from his jacket. I bent to pick it up and nearly had a convulsion.

Fifty Shades of Grey.

I was so fucking delighted. A true stick to wallop the living be-fuck out of him.

When he returned, reeking of nicotine enough to make me, a smoker, gag, I prepared my best shot. At school, in the days when the clergy could beat you with impunity, and often with approval, they liked to lecture at length about dirty books.

Pronounced *doirty*,

as if they all originated from Dublin.

Prime contenders were:

Joyce, of course, though you'd have thought a medal would be more fitting for attempting to get a thrill from *Finnegans Wake*,

Edna O'Brien,

J. P. Donleavy,

Ian Fleming,

and a series of soft to softest porn novels, all with the name *Angelique* in them.

Before I could launch, he signalled for fresh pints, said,

"I'm sorry for your friend."

And before I could say anything, he added,

"Even though he was a Protestant."

There are times — not many so much any more, but enough — that sheer hereditary hatred will stun me. Malachy had trained, if such a term as *train* can be applied to the priests of his generation, but fuck, he spent seven years in a seminary doing something besides playing hurling and bad-mouthing Brits.

Liturgy, theology, the Latin Mass: surely they would have dented even his thick skin.

Seemingly not.

324

One time, he'd told me that sending silver paper to the African missions, mad as it seems, was a widespread practice.

I'd asked in dismay,

"What the fuck for?"

Cross me heart, waiting for a half-sane answer. He'd told me,

"Gollywogs like shiny things."

Now he asked,

"Your friend, Savile, was it?"

A sly dig at the Jimmy Savile scandal rocking the BBC, but maybe I gave him too much guile credit.

I hissed,

"Stewart."

He shrugged, laying into the fresh pint.

"Not an Irish lad, then."

Jesus.

Maybe blunt trauma would kickstart him. I said,

"The shotgun blast tore off his face."

Unfazed, he said,

"I know. I've hunted rabbits in me time."

Enough.

I stood up and he grabbed my jacket, cried,

"Jack, Jesus, don't go, I need your help."

Truth to tell, I hesitated. Time of the Priest, a nasty, vicious case involving child abuse, Malachy had been on the accusatory hook and nigh decimated. He'd begged for my help and I'd managed to free him of the stain. Was he grateful?

Yeah, right, along the lines of Oscar's

no good deed shall go unpunished.

Too, he never, like fucking ever, missed an opportunity to

slag,

slander,

and, as the kids say,

diss

me in every form of religious viciousness at his yellowed fingertips. So the temptation to go,

Go fuck your unholy self

was paramount.

I sighed, Jesus, almost like my mother, who could have sighed for Ireland and frequently did. I'd say Lord Rest Her, but not even the Almighty has that alchemy.

His gratitude was almost worse than his bile. He gushed,

"Christ, Jack, thanks, thanks a million."

I snarled,

"Hey, I didn't say I'd help. You hear me say I'd do that?"

He nearly smiled. The bollix. I was sitting, so he was halfway home, now he'd but to nail the deal. The barman, unbidden, brought two Jamesons, said to Malachy,

"On the house, Father."

He grunted as if such was only to be expected, said to me,

"*Sláinte mhaith.*"

I left the toast and the drink cold, asked,

"Get to it."

The Jay immediately lit up his cheeks, giving that bar-room tan beloved by reality TV. His eyes shone and he began.

"The Church says we have to tighten our belts, the public are not giving as generously as of yore."

Of fucking yore.

Jesus, had he morphed into Darby O'Gill? My face must have shown my ire — a good word to add to yore, I guess.

I felt the rush of anger, spat,

"Christ, people can't feed their families, pay mortgages, and you expect them to continue paying your wages? Wake up, Padre, the country is dying from poverty."

Not a stir out of him.

He said,

"Your shout."

I didn't shout — that is, for the next round. I asked in a quiet tone,

"How much were you needing?"

He said,

"Well, you got the big payoff from the dead Prod."

Incredulous, I asked,

"How did you know?"

He laughed, not from humour but pure unadulterated spite, said,

"The bank fellah. I'm his priest."

Jesus, no wonder we were fucked. I took a deep breath, asked,

"How much were you estimating you could wrench from me?"

The drinks had woven their malicious alchemy and he had a cockiness that I remembered well from days when the clergy ruled like feudal lords. He said,

"You know, your mother, Lord rest the poor woman, wouldn't like me to be out on the street."

And came as close to a wallop to the head as it gets. My mother was *never* the route to go. I said,

"I'll go the bank, see what I can get. I don't suppose you'd take a cheque?"

He gave me a look of utter devilment, said,

"Cash keeps us all afloat, wouldn't you say?"

I could have said a lot of things, but, to him, like a wasted prayer on a wasted overgrown forgotten grave. I got up to leave and he said,

"God knows, Jack, but you're not the worst."

A blessing from the inferno.

Sister Wendy, Britain's favourite nun, is eighty-two. She reveals,

"I have a cold heart. People never meant much to me. I was a nasty child with no emotions."

I read this in the paper, the *Irish Independent*, as I waited for Reardon to show. We'd to meet at seven, Tuesday evening. He'd suggested McSwiggan's, said,

"I feel the need to see that tree growing in the centre of the pub."

Fucking with me.

I wanted to ask him for a job for the cop's daughter and hoped then to find where Kelly was and, as Liam Neeson said, track her down and kill her. Nice thoughts to run as I read of a cold-hearted nun. Obama was re-elected, but the big news here was the next Irish ambassador might be,

wait for it,
breath held,
Clinton.
Our new Bono and John Kennedy in one. We hated
Bono due to the whole tax gig. Clinton seemed to love
us as much as we did him. Michael Winner, the film
director, in his final column for the *Sunday Times*,
wrote,
   "I'm a totally insane film director, writer, producer,
silk-shirt cleaner, bad-tempered, totally ridiculous example
of humanity in deep shit."
   Still, if it came to the wire, who'd you have a pint
with?
   Him or Sister Wendy?

A mammoth man approached my table. I'd just got
what looked like the perfect pint: the head was so
creamy, so still, it seemed a sin to touch it. The man's
shadow fell across that head. I looked up, he was
seriously steroid. And you could see *road rage* dance in
his eyes. I hoped to fuck I didn't owe this megaton
anything. He was wearing a suit, swear to Christ, or,
rather, a fabulously expensive cloth had been draped
over his form and he just let hang.
   He asked,
   "You Taylor?"
   I wanted to go Hollywood, snarl,
   Depends who's asking.
   But, seriously?
   I said,
   "Yeah."

And to cream off the surreal element, he spoke into his cuff, like all the movies, said,

"Clear,"

and moved to a table close by. It was so fucking deliciously lunatic, I could almost have appreciated it. A moment later, Reardon sauntered in, dressed in Silicon Valley chic:

chinos, trainers and the ubiquitous T with a logo:

WIRED TO THE POGUES.

OK.

He smiled, asked,

"May I sit?"

I said,

"You probably own the place by now, but sure."

He was immediately attended by the barman, who asked,

"Mr Reardon, what can we get you?"

In true ego vein, he never looked at him, said,

"Same as Mr Taylor here, and, oh, rustle up some fries with curry sauce."

No need to mention the kitchen was long closed. He'd get the fries if the guy had to run up to Supermac's. I finally took a draught, said,

"*Sláinte mhaith.*"

He said,

"You wanted something?"

I told him, the cop's daughter, a job? He didn't hesitate, said,

"Sure."

I was surprised, went,

"Really, just like that? I mean, don't you want any details?"

He finally got his pint, drank deep, made a sound of joy, said,

"In my world, all is joy and light."

I looked at the mega bodyguard, said,

"He part of the . . . joy?"

Reardon gave a long scrutiny, then,

"This is my movie, Jack. Don't you get that? You're just part of the plot."

His fries came, the curry sauce giving off a strong aroma. He ate them noisily. I asked,

"How is Kelly?"

He pushed the fries aside, burped, said — and I was later to discover parts of what he told me were true. That was his game, sprinkle all the lies with nibbles of truth — he said,

"See, thing with Kelly is, she gets . . . hyped."

Laughed.

"Jacked, if you like, then burns out, we ship her off, get her serious EST, and blast the hell out her memories, then, good as new, she's out, ready to boogie."

I said,

"Part of the boogie being murder."

He signalled for the bar guy, said,

"Two shots of Black Bush."

To me,

"The tattoo dude, he's now saying, gee, guess what, the needle in the other dude's eye, pure accident."

I felt the bile rise, asked,

"Stewart, my friend, he part of the . . . memory loss?"

He said,

"Bottoms up."

The shot downed, he said,

"Stewart is history and now your friend's daughter, she has a bright future. All is hunky dory, isn't it?"

The velvet threat.

I got up to leave, didn't touch the Bushmills, said,

"Appreciate your time."

He was staring at the shot glass, then shook himself, said,

"Thing to remember, Jack, about my movie?"

I waited.

"In the final edit, lots of shit gets, like, you know, on the cutting-room floor."

I said,

"Jesus, Mary and Joe Cocker."

He laughed, asked,

"You speak American now?"

I let him savour it, then,

"From Series One of *Damages*."

He took my glass, turned it over the fries, watched the whiskey muddle over the curry sauce, dribble over the side of the plate, begin to drip to the wooden floor, said,

"It's all there, Jack. Some of us, the followers, we're TV, get maybe one series."

I was tired of him, his bullshit sermons, asked,

"And you're the movie mogul, right?"

He smiled, shook his head.

"No, Jack. Smell the coffee, I'm the money guy."

35

"You think they can convict her," I said. "Motive and opportunity, prior solicitation to murder, plus the jury won't like her."

"Because?"

"Because she's what my mother would have called cheap. She's too pretty, too made up, too blonde, lot of attitude, drinks to excess, probably does dope, sleeps around."

"Sounds like a great date," I said.

Robert Parke, *Widow's Walk*

"He would never again tempt innocence, he would be good."

Oscar Wilde, *The Picture of Dorian Gray*

Lewis Hyde wrote about John Berryman, and it's a wee stretch to see it as the Modern Ireland, whereas irony was once riding point to our deep abiding sense of humour. Now, as Hyde said,

"Irony is only of use once."

Irony has only emergency use. Carried over time, it is the voice of the trapped who have come to enjoy their cage.

Fuck, I hated that to be true. And as I waited to meet with Tremlin, the cop whose daughter Reardon said he'd employ, I seethed over the newly published Richard Burton diaries.

The critics had always lumped the *Celtic hellraisers,*
O'Toole,
Harris,
as if there was romance in drink-to-lunacy shenanigans.
Christ on a bike.

Burton wrote that he despised the Irish, everything about them, *their posturing, the silly soft accents, their literature, their genius for self-advertisement, their mock belligerence.*

Pause.

Their obvious charm.

It was small comfort that we'd beaten the bejaysus out of the Welsh in the Nations Cup.

While I waited for the cop, a guy came into Garavan's, made a beeline for me, offered,

"Want to buy a book of poems?"

He had that half-insane expression of a patient newly released from the mental hospital or a recent convert to veganism. Which is much the same thing. I asked,

"Who are they by?"

He seemed to think that was the most foolish question he'd heard in many's the day, petulated,

"Meself."

Sure, I could have asked,

And you are?

Went,

"How much?"

"Eighteen euros, and two for twenty-five."

I bought one, the volume titled,

The Abortion Collection.

On the back it declared,

"Do judge by the cover."

It's a spoof, a joke.

So maybe my thoughts of irony were premature. Tremlin arrived, looking hale and *happy?* Guards did happy? He ordered from the barman, breezed over to me, his hand extended, said,

"Gotta give it up for you, mate, you delivered."

I did?

I gave the humble smile, related in a pure way to the grimace. He sat, continued,

"Jesus H. My missus is over the moon. A job with Reardon, she'd been sure our little one would be emigrating like all the rest."

Pints came.

He raised his, smiled.

"*Sláinte agus go raibh míle maith agat.*"

Staying in the humble mode, I said,

"Glad to be of help."

He reached in his jacket, produced a black leather folder, asked,

"You ever hear of the Refuge?"

Unless it was Johnny Duhan's new album.

He continued,

"The rich — and I mean the seriously fucking loaded, the type you and I only wet-dream about — they have their own very private hospitals. For addictions, sex crimes, all the shite the tabloids would kill for, they've created their own treatment centres, and the Refuge is the very best. You ever hear of Gormanston?"

"Yeah, a boarding school for boys, run by . . . Franciscans?"

"Right, Ireland's very own Eton."

Perish the thought.

He said,

"In County Meath, about five miles up the road from this posh school, is the Refuge."

He tapped the folder.

"Map and assorted shite in here, plus . . ."

Waited.

The big flourish:

produced a warrant card, said,

"Special Branch, and it's even got your name on it."

I was impressed.

He held it out to me, cautioned,

"One time only, Jack, that's all it's valid for, else . . ."

Let it trail off.

I took it and felt, Jesus, what?

Ferocious regret. If only, fuck, I hadn't been thrown out of the Force, would I have gone on . . . would . . .?

And shut it off, said,

"This is bloody great, thank you."

He motioned with his glass and more pints were built. He said,

"Don't wait too long to use it. The *patients*, especially the high-priority ones, they tend to be moved after a few weeks."

He then moved on to hurling, the Galway team and our hope of the All-Ireland next year.

After I left him, I took a walk down through the town with my Special Branch ID, the book of poems, and felt, in a jagged way, I was most of what you might call the Irish contradiction.

Ridge felt enormous guilt over Stewart's legacy. Who knew he'd amassed so much? She'd sent a cheque off to Our Lady's Hospital, Crumlin; the work they did with children would uplift the most grizzled cynic.

A light-blue 2008 Ford Focus 1.8. By pure coincidence she saw it slashed in price and, on a whim, bought it.

Then the guilt eased. Stewart had been nagging her to buy a car. 'Course, with the money she now had, she could have bought two of them. The seller had explained about mileage, even pulled the bonnet up, telling her about fuel gauges. She listened with feigned interest. They both knew . . .

she liked the colour.

Friday, she finished work early, decided to take the car for a decent workout, familiarize herself with the stick shift.

Heading out of the city, she figured she'd go as far as the new motorway bridge just outside Loughrea. Traffic was relatively light as she accelerated towards the bridge. At the stairs on the left-hand side of the bridge, a young man struggled as he made it to the top. He had to stop, wipe the sweat from his brow. The large jagged piece of concrete had left deep ridges on his hands and he muttered,

"Aw, fuck."

Looked around, as if his mother would appear and clip his ear for cursing. On the bridge now, he was alone. He'd timed it every day for a week and knew almost to the minute the time when the bridge was deserted. He looked out over the rim, a grey BMW glided under him like a shark.

"Shite."

He thought,

That one would have made a fierce bang.

Sighing, grunting, he hefted the concrete on to the rim, nearly lost it, and just managed to hold the block back. He had seen this so many times in his mind, it had to be exactly right.

The colour.

God alone knew why, but the car had to be the colour of the one in his imagination.

Light blue.

36

"*The weather will continue bad, he says. There will be more calamities, more death, more despair. Not the slightest indication of a change anywhere . . . We must get into step, a lockstep toward the prison of death. There is no escape. The weather will not change.*"

Henry Miller, *Tropic of Cancer*

I stayed in a small hotel off O'Connell Street. I'd hired a car; business was brisk and I had to settle for a Corolla. It was all they had left in a black shade and dark I wanted to be. Come evening, I was restless, being out of Galway. I went to Madigan's, had a few pints and failed to hear a single Dublin accent. All seemed to be from Eastern Europe and, indeed, our main street in our capital city looked more like a repressed satellite state. Grey, grimy, dope-infested, grim. Spent an hour in Chapters, the huge secondhand bookstore, and found three of Derek Raymond's Factory novels. Apt for the way I was feeling.

On the road early, I wanted to get the job done before the hospital got full neon. Dressed dull:

black slacks,
black shoes,
off-white shirt,
an excuse for a bad tie,
and my Garda all-weather.

My bedraggled face would be accessory enough for the Special Branch papers.

Once I found my way out of the city, the drive was almost pleasant. The radio had a nice blend of Mark

Roberts and Gretchen Peters. Kept my mood low. The directions were good and I found myself heading up a tree-lined avenue in little over an hour. The Refuge was one of the old Anglo-Irish mansions, restored and renovated. Mainly, they'd have put in heating.

Got out of the car, surveyed for a moment. A garage to the left seemed to be for staff and there were up to ten vehicles. I headed for the front entrance.

Inside it was quiet with that suppressed hospital vibe of things unseen. An attractive woman, late thirties, manned reception.

In my days in the Guards, even we'd believed,

don't ever fuck with Special Branch.

The woman was sniffy until I flashed the ID.

The change was heartening. She didn't pale but definitely faltered. Said,

"I'll have to get Dr James."

I stared at her, said nothing and she echoed,

"Right . . . um, I'll do that so."

Did some jigging with the switchboard, then,

"Dr James will be here forthwith."

Forthwith.

Who the fuck talked like that?

But indeed, forthwith or not, he was there in jig time. A big man, in his fifties, even his beard was big. No white coat for this chappie. Tweeds ruled the day and the man.

He boomed,

"Let's take it over here."

Meaning the lobby, beside a bay window. We sat, he commanded,

344

"Papers."

The guy was used to hopping staff. He peered at my ID and I knew I had to act, asked,

"You have a problem with the Branch?"

Letting insinuation, accusation, suspicion, run riot over the words. He almost flinched, tried to regroup, asked,

"What do you want?"

I gave the hard-arse smile, said,

"My ID, firstly."

Get some ground rules down.

He said,

"We don't usually have this sort of scrutiny."

I stared at him, asked,

"How often do you have someone of Mr Reardon's power and . . . *resources*, need your *help?*"

His eyes flinched and I had the money shot. Pushed,

"Rehab and security, the only two growth resources in these dark days. Place like this costs a mighty load of euros to run, and a sponsor of . . . unlimited assets."

I stood up, said,

"I'd like to see her now."

He stood and, almost smoothly, backed away from me, physical distance in lieu of eroding authority. He said,

"You must understand . . ."

I put up my hand, enjoying it a bit, said,

"Whoa, Doc, drop the imperatives, OK?"

He did, said,

"We've had to administer some therapy."

I laughed, said,

"The old electric-shock treatment?"

Shook his head, said,

"Oh, no, we don't do that, we have MST."

Like a car warranty. He waited, then,

"It's memory-suppressor therapy."

I asked,

"You still apply the voltage?"

"Well, yes . . ."

I said,

"Same shite, different label."

He was about to protest. I cut through, said,

"I want to see her now."

He considered many options, none of them ridding him of me, which is what he most desired, said,

"Very well, but I must caution you, she isn't yet very responsive."

Led me to an upstairs room, did the gig with many keys and opened the door.

I grabbed his arm, said,

"Go get yourself some coffee."

I moved in, pulled the door behind me. Kelly was seated by the large window, looking out on a deserted garden. Dressed in a white tracksuit, she was absolutely still. The room resembled a luxurious hotel, save for the locks on the outside. I said,

"Hi, babe."

No response.

I grabbed the desk chair, pulled it over, sat right next to her face. Her face was completely devoid of expression. I said,

"I was in your apartment."

Nothing.

Continued,

"Found some very impressive volumes of Wilde, and guess what?"

Her eyes flickered, barely, but something going on — or inwards, rather. I said,

"One volume really caught my interest. It was signed by your father."

A faint stir in the eyes and a tiny movement in her shoulders. I sat back, as if seeing the book, said,

"Tell you, Kell, it was a beautiful piece of work."

Let her hear that past tense, waited a beat, said,

"And fuck, the way that sucker burned."

She spat in my face, her hands going for my eyes. I slapped her back, said,

"Whoa, that's some miraculous recovery."

Then, as if a light went out, she slumped in her chair, even let her mouth sag, but couldn't quite prevent a sly smile race across the corners of her mouth. I stood, said,

"I'm going to give you a countdown, when you eventually walk, and Reardon has covered your arse in all the ways that matter. A certain number of days, you'll turn around and I'll be there, give you the same chance you gave my friend Stewart."

I headed for the door, banged on it and, as it opened, heard,

"How many days?"

I gave her my winning smile, said,

"Thirty-three."

★ ★ ★

The boy had the concrete slab finely balanced, beads of perspiration burst on his forehead from exertion and high excitement. He looked up the road and nearly crapped himself. A light-blue car was coming.

Ridge was uncertain whether to turn for home now or make the turn after the bridge. On pure whim, she said,

"Let's see what you got."

Her foot pushed down on the accelerator, she felt a burst of joy as the car hurled towards the bridge. It was the first break in the blanket of grief that had enshrouded her.

The boy focused, shouted,

"Blue rules!"

Crows perched on a lone tree near the motorway, startled by the grinding crash of metal and exploding glass, hurled into the air like tiny stealth bombers above the bridge, their glass eyes registering only what might be deemed scavengings. Their harsh cawing like a screech heard behind a confession gone rogue.

Ken Bruen was born in Galway, Ireland. After turning down a place at RADA, and completing a doctorate in Metaphysics, he spent twenty-five years as an English teacher in Africa, Japan, Southeast Asia and South America. An unscheduled stint in a Brazilian prison where he suffered physical and mental abuse spurred him to write and, after a brief spell teaching in London, he returned to Galway, where he now lives with his daughter.

Headstone

Ken Bruen

Evil has many guises. Jack Taylor has encountered most of them but nothing before has ever truly terrified him until a group called Headstone rears its ugly head. An elderly priest is viciously beaten until nearly dead. A special needs boy is brutally attacked. A series of seemingly random, insane events even has the Guards shaken.

Accepting the power of Headstone, Jack realises that in order to fight back he must relinquish the remaining shreds of what has made him human — knowledge that may have come too late to prevent an act of such ferocious evil that the whole country would be changed forever — and in the worst way.

With awful clarity, Jack knows not only might he be powerless to stop it but that he may not have the grit needed to even face it.

ISBN 978-0-7531-9122-4 (hb)
ISBN 978-0-7531-9123-1 (pb)

Blitz

Ken Bruen

Detective Sergeant Brant is tough and uncompromising, as sleazy and ruthless as the villains he's out to get.
His violent methods may be questionable, but he
always gets results.

A psychopath has started a killing spree across London.
Calling himsel "The Blitz", his weapon of choice is a
workman's hammer. And his victims are all cops.

The police squad are desperate to catch the killer
before he catches up with them. And Brant is top of his
list . . .

ISBN 978-0-7531-8916-0 (hb)
ISBN 978-0-7531-8917-7 (pb)

The Devil

Ken Bruen

America — the land of opportunity, a place where economic prosperity beckons: but not for PI Jack Taylor, who's just been refused entry. Disappointed and bitter, he thinks that an encounter with an over-friendly stranger in an airport bar is the least of his problems. Except that this stranger seems to know rather more than he should about Jack. Jack thinks no more of their meeting and resumes his old life in Galway. But when he's called to investigate a student murder — connected to an elusive Mr K — he remembers the man from the airport. Is the stranger really is who he says he is? After several more murders and too many coincidental encounters, Jack believes he may have met his nemesis. But why has he been chosen? And could he really have taken on the devil himself?

ISBN 978-0-7531-8878-1 (hb)
ISBN 978-0-7531-8879-8 (pb)

London Boulevard

Ken Bruen

When Mitchell is released from prison after serving three years for a vicious attack he doesn't remember, he reluctantly finds himself caught up with Robert Gant, a ruthless lowlife with violent plans.

Attempting to stay out of Gant's way, Mitchell finds work as a handyman at the mansion of a faded movie actress. When she eagerly plies him with cash, cars and sex, Mitch starts to wonder if even this job comes with a catch.

But it isn't long before Mitchell's violent past catches up with him. When people close to him start getting hurt, Mitchell is forced to act, and take brutal revenge on those who've stolen his life . . .

ISBN 978-0-7531-8870-5 (hb)
ISBN 978-0-7531-8871-2 (pb)